Woman of

Michaela Beckett

Fishers of Folk Publishing

Published by
Fishers of Folk Publishing,
14 High Street, Lakenheath, Brandon, Suffolk, IP27 9JX

First Edition

Characters and events are purely fictional, any similarities to persons either
living or dead is coincidental, not intended by the author.

ISBN
978-0-9576385-0-1

Printed in England, 2013

This book is dedicated to my dearest daughters, Aeryn and Jemima. You are the light and joy of each day to me and this book was written while remembering the tender days of carrying you both in my arms as babes, I will carry you in my heart as you grow, always.

Also to my husband, Nathan. Your support, understanding and excitement has been a fuel to the writing fire, thank you.

To my first reader and my biggest fan, Kathleen. You spent almost as much time re-reading this book as I did to get it as it is now, so thank you from the bottom of my heart.

To my big sister, Hannah, for always cheering me on and for being the strong woman that I am immensely proud of! Also to my dad for his constant supply of help and information, you have been invaluable to the process of getting this book from plan to print!

To my mother, who I will always await as the father did his prodigal son. Love never fails and never gives up, I too will never give up on you.

To my dear friends and family. You listened to me talk about this book and prayed for me when the going got rough, I love you all so much and would be lost without you!

To Flea, a kindred spirit and the fellow adventurer who discovered the beautiful Abergele and Gwyrch Castle with me. Camping in the foothills of the stunning scenery it provided and getting stuck on the side of a cliff with me in the pouring rain, it has been a wild ride but you made it fun!

I also dedicate this book to my Saviour and King, without whom I would not know how to love and forgive.

Thank you must go to those at Gwyrch castle trust, who are working to preserve the stunning and captivating building which inspired this book.

Also a massive thank you to Si Moore of Spirit Photography for the stunning cover photo of Gwyrch Castle, and for his patience in our preparations for the making of the cover. Keep taking photographs, you are incredibly talented!

Table of Contents

Chapter 1 – Take Flight

When the fair of face become a king,
So a new world will be ushered in,
Brother agin brother and kin before kin,
To undo an age old sin,
A fair one born with a simple tell,
To see through eyes looking into Hell,
Before the time to be restored,
The child will break the dissonant chord,
Then be drawn blood from own blood,
Will cleanse the land by filth and flood,
In time will bring a peace unknown,
A reunited kingdom's thrones,
And once again man shall stand,
To rule before united land.

Xandian Prophesy

Autumn

She felt her heart pounding inside her chest, like a beacon giving her hiding place away. She felt Etana's milky warm breath on her cold skin, stroked the baby's downy black hair and tried not to concentrate on the rushing of panic in her ears. He was close by; she could feel it. Fellyn swept the thick branches of bushes apart, slowly peering into the shaded clearing she had begun to sleep in before Luca had started to pace and growl. Luca was a reliable guard, she was intensely protective of the little family especially Etana, perhaps because her

6

bond was so strong with Fellyn that she felt like another mother to the child. Fellyn had found the dog abandoned and starving to near death in the woods when out picking fruit from the trees, she had sat with the animal night and day; when others had told her she was a fool for trying, she had known in her heart that the dog had a strong will and would survive, tame. It had been a struggle, but Luca had recovered fully and become a vital asset to the Kellack household. Through their short time, Fellyn had learned to trust the dog and knew that if Luca was bothered now, that Jared must be close by, close enough for the dog to smell him and begin to show distress. Fellyn wanted to run but knew that if she were caught in a chase, she would lose. Jared would undoubtedly be faster and he knew the forests close to Tebel well, better than she herself and the last thing Fellyn needed was to get lost due to panic.

The mother closed her eyes, breathed deeply and looked at the tiny bundle she had strapped to her body, expecting Etana to be sleeping, she was surprised to see two big eyes staring up at her, Etana's eyes were the colour of the sky after a storm; so deep they were practically purple. The pupil in her left eye ran into the iris like a little river, making Etana's little face striking and even more beautiful. Fellyn smiled at her daughter and held her closer; she pulled the hood from her cloak over her head and backed further into the bushes. She sat down slowly to make as little noise as possible, cringing as she snapped a twig with her leg and froze, waiting to hear any noise; something, anything to tell her if her hiding place was known. Luca lay somewhere to Fellyn's right under the main trunk of the bush, her ears forward, her hind legs poised ready to spring if needed. Fellyn relaxed and hushed Etana as the baby began to wriggle and whimper slightly, Fellyn put her little finger into the baby's mouth and let her suck for a few minutes. The little glen seemed clear, so she allowed herself to lean back into the pile of dead leaves on the floor and shut her eyes. She was exhausted.

Jared had heard noises up ahead and could smell the smoke from a recent campfire being doused. He could tell Fellyn had been through this way by the shape of the slight tracks he had seen a way back, one of a human and a set belonging to an animal, Luca. The dog was his biggest concern, it had never liked him and he knew it. He would have liked nothing more than to shoot it when out hunting, to claim it was accidental, but he could see how much Fellyn loved the animal and it pained his heart to think of taking away her biggest comfort. Jared could also not deny that Luca was helpful in assisting him in catching meat. He was infamous in the village of Tebel for being the best hunter, and prided himself in being able to provide meat for several families in the village including his own mother and sisters, an elderly couple who used to look after him and his siblings as children and also the chief's wife and children, when the chief was away of course. The chief often went to the closest town, Cabaro to discuss "important matters", although Jared often wondered if that was out of self-importance rather than necessity, but he enjoyed providing for Rhia and her children regardless. Tebel, their humble village, sat near the port town Cabaro, in the southern-most parts of Xandia, a small country with rich lands and good people. Each of the towns and villages in Xandia had a chief who was educated in Varose, the city of the clouds, situated high on the side of Mount Varen, and each chief was selected from their training group and sworn in to the High council; a democratic group who had been in control for many years now, bringing prosperity to their lands. There was a head of the High council, who had final decision making status, the man currently filling the post was Darue, an intelligent man with very little charisma or charm, but he led the high council well. Cassius was Tebel's chief, he left for Cabaro regularly and Varose less so, he was a rotund man who got under Jared's skin, and who watched him like a hawk without cause.

Jared stepped into the little clearing he had come to, looked around for signs of life and sat down to listen. He would find Fellyn and when he did she would be sorry. How dare she leave him, and for what reason? But as soon as the thoughts of punishing Fellyn crossed his mind, Jared felt sick to his stomach. He knew it was from his own anger that Fellyn had grown cold to him, and that he must have finally scared her away. The only problem was, he didn't really understand why she had run from him now. Breathing in the smell of the forest, he remembered his wife's face. The smell of the leaves on the trees as they changed colour from emerald to gold and mahogany, the heavy air bringing with it the possibility of rain and the sweet smell of apples. Fellyn liked to roast these in autumn with herbs and serve it with a pig from his mother's farm. He closed his eyes and let his mind wander to Fellyn's cooking, her gentle hands and tender heart, he allowed himself a minute to feel sorry for himself for acting the way he did sometimes, and then walked away from the clearing as he pulled at his thick black hair in anguish.

Fellyn sat in the thick bushes and waited, she had seen Jared's thick boots move from the middle of the large space, out West in pursuit of her small group, but he was headed in a loop back to their village. She sighed quietly, waited until nightfall and nursed Etana in the warmth of the bush. It was itchy and harsh on her delicate skin so Fellyn had wrapped material from her own dress around the baby and sewed her skirts together into trousers to make it easier to walk and run. She had been sewing when the arrow set her house ablaze and her needle and thread had been pinned to her dress before she had left. She sent Luca out into the clearing, watching for the slightest twitch in the animal's strong stance. The dog paused and then sniffed the ground and sat facing the east path. Fellyn slipped out of the bushes and called to Luca with a whisper, standing side by side they moved gracefully through the clearing to the Eastern path, followed it for about a hundred yards and then moved into the heart of the thicker trees, seeking an un-trodden route to the mountains.

Many years before...

Tehya smiled at the young girl in front of her, the thick locks of black hair matted around her grubby young face. She looked into the determined brown eyes of a girl about ten years of age and saw a soul much older. This child had endured many hardships and was in need of care. She had no memory of her past, her family or how she had come to be in the forest lands; all she knew was that she had once lived in the valley of tall mountains, Moranye.

Tehya took the girl's hand and showed her around the small cottage, teaching her how to find things she would need and telling her how to take care of herself. She took her to the living area, where the girl saw a small dog curled up at the feet of an old cosy chair, she looked at the animal and asked Tehya what his name was.

"No, darlin' he not be mine. That little lad come from the hills like yerself, he just be passing through, see."

"Must I go too, like the dog will?" The child looked into the wise woman's face and felt her cheeks burn, she was shamed to be relying upon a stranger and wished she knew where home was.

"That be your path, little lass. You decide that time when you be good and ready."

Tehya smiled at the girl, tonight she would let her rest, she had come a long way to find help, and Tehya's cottage had been the closest building to the forest. Yes, the girl should sleep a-while and be put to work come morning.

The girl held Tehya's hand tightly and smiled shyly as she was led to a little room where she saw a bed covered with a stitched blanket in an array of colour, she liked the smell of the room; it was sweet and welcoming. As she turned the slight corner she stood and watched

10

Tehya busy herself with a folded blanket of pale blue-green wool. She grabbed hold of the corners opposite Tehya and helped fold it into shape for the second bed, it was a small sack-cloth covering straw underneath, the blanket would serve as a buffer to the hard material holding the straw in. Tehya laid the folded blanket upon the bedding and fetched another warm sheet, this one an emerald green. The girl began to remove her dress and slipped into the little bed, it was warm and dry, and to the eyes of one so lost, the best bed in the world. Tehya glanced at the girl's tiny frame, she was underfed alright. Tehya smiled at the child, patted her head and slipped out of the little room, off to finish her daily tasks before supper and bed. The girl lay in the bed, she understood that she was demanding a lot of the woman, but she was relieved to be safe and warm at last, it had been cold in the trees and she had not known how to find food or shelter. She sighed, if only she could remember her name, maybe then she could figure out how she had come to be lost in the trees. As sleep took over her weary body, she whispered a little prayer and wondered if she would cease to exist if she could never remember who she really was.

Tehya peered into the room and saw the girl sleeping soundly, yes; she was in need of a good woman to show her an honest way of life. Her name, though. Tehya stared into the little face and saw a mark upon the porcelain skin behind her delicate ear, in the perfect shape of a fish. "*Fellyn*," she whispered, that suited the little dear, for she had been left to be in control of her own path so young in the icy cool of winter in the Moranye mountains. Tomorrow would bring a new life for the girl. And as Tehya blew out the candle and rolled over to sleep, Fellyn dreamed of frozen streams and a deep, deep snow on tall mountains.

Present day

Fellyn woke to the sound of the birds singing, she opened her eyes and sat upright, how could she have slept so soundly without even planning her resting place? She had intended to stop briefly to feed Etana, not to rest, but sleep she had. The little baby was sweating, breathing slowly and snuffling gently.

"Oh, how I love you dear one" she whispered to her daughter. Fellyn looked up to see Luca drinking from the stream beside them, her long fur draping into the running water, she paddled in the water for a while, then climbed the banks and went to lay down beside the bundled baby that Fellyn had just laid down. Etana was now awake and cooing, she sucked on her own little hands as she kicked around in the leaves. Luca licked the baby's toes and laid her big head down beside her, curling her furry body around the child like a barrier. Fellyn smiled at the pair and went to collect some water in her wineskin. She kicked her bare toes in the cold water as she scooped some up to drink, and then undressed to wash. She was lucky that water was plentiful here, she would not have made it so far without easy access to the stream, but she would only use the shallow parts. Fellyn shivered at the thought of deeper water and saw a face in her mind that she had come to realise was part of her unknown past, but this face had looked at her through ice, cold and hard as she had looked back into it. She did not know this face, but she had seen this in her dreams and felt a familiarity despite not knowing whose it was. After rubbing her body down with a little water and dipping her long black hair to rub it clean, she slipped her clothes back on and felt the warmth of the sun on her neck, she tied her hair back into a loose bun and called the dog to her side. She needed to find some food to eat, but she also needed to know which direction her hunter was headed.

Fellyn rolled up the long legs of her sewn dress and strode into the path with Luca beside her, she tiptoed through the debris of fallen branches and dead leaves and crouched in the shade behind a large tree. Fellyn sent Luca forward with a wave of her hand, instructing the dog to lay down when she had reached a place with good cover but placed well to give chase. Silently they waited, even though she wasn't far away, Fellyn hated having to leave Etana while she hunted, but they all needed to eat. Whilst Etana did not need food yet, Fellyn herself needed enough to keep her strong for two since she was feeding the baby around the clock. She also knew that it was important for her and Luca to establish firm companionship and better hunting abilities, as they would need more of it in the harder months of winter that were approaching. Fellyn did not have a plan, her decision to leave was under pressure. She had been sewing a blanket for Etana in the dark of evening, candle flickering beside her, humming a song. She had been trying to picture her mother's face and seeing only Tehya's.

*Fellyn had heard the firing of a bow and saw the arrow beside her left arm, she threw herself on the floor, not allowing time to look at her attacker, and froze while her heart beat furiously, sweat beaded her pale forehead and she crawled to the little basket on the floor. **Etana**. She grabbed the bundle, her body as flattened as she felt was possible and shimmied across the floor. Who was it? What was going on? She felt her spine tingle at the presence of someone nearby, she heard a cold laugh and some grabbed her neck, pinching at her skin and pulling her hair. She could smell the drink on his breath and the blood on his hands, **Jared**. She stood slowly with the tug of his hands upwards, still with her back to him, the tiny bundle pressed tight to her bosom, the baby stirred and whimpered. **Oh God, please take care of us**!*

She felt his grip lessen and fall, he scraped his nails across her bare neck and as Fellyn waited for a blow to her head, she felt his hand release her. She closed her eyes and stood frozen, waiting, waiting. When she opened them she saw no one but Luca, teeth bared and hackles raised. She stood, breathing heavily, looking into the eyes of Luca and seeing her own frightened reflection, just seeing Luca had scared Jared away and she thanked God for blessing her with the dog all those years ago. She turned to check he had really left, hurried to pack a small bag of necessary items and sat again, and waited until she heard nothing for a minute. Had he really gone? Fellyn was unsure, she did not want to stay for him, but worried about leaving. As she stood by the stove, she heard a familiar sound, she held Etana closer and turned, fire. He had sent a burning arrow into their wooden house and her little sewn blanket was already aflame, she darted away and fumbled in shock. Another. Fellyn gasped and turned to the door, seeing her exit blocked by yet another fire, and seeing no escape she began to panic, in those few seconds, her instincts kicked in, she ran to the window and climbed out, with her small pack strapped to her back and Etana to her front, she would have to leave the rest behind, Luca sprang out after her. The two ran into the darkness of the orchard and darted under cover, he hadn't seen them! Fellyn shivered, glanced back at her flaming home, and ran away into the thick trees.

Fellyn heard the creak of twigs as Luca slowly stood, she had been day-dreaming, remembering their last night at home. Jared had frightened her beyond return and she had feared for the baby. Jared had fired his bow at her home, *their* home. What could have possessed him to do so? As she let out her breath she felt her heart sag, she was still in love with the man who had tried to kill her that night. Yet something about the attack stirred and worried her, it was unlike Jared to act without any previous talk or anger at her and she had never before been so open and vulnerable, caught off guard. That had been her final incentive to leave, the fear for her own and her child's life. Nothing was coming for her daughter whilst she still breathed, not even the girl's own father. Fellyn turned her head slowly to the side as she saw something move in the corner of her brown eyes, Luca was motionless on the other side of the tree, the rabbit had not seen them. With her hand down beside her legs she pointed Luca forward, the dog crawled away from the tree to a spot behind the rabbit, they had put the animal in-between the huntresses. Swift as an arrow both Luca and Fellyn moved. Fellyn stood and darted at the animal, it turned and dashed backwards, away from the over gestured movements Fellyn had used, Luca sprung and began a high speed chase through the trees behind the rabbit which was darting left and right in an attempt to lose the large dog on its heels. By using their opening trap, they had given

14

Luca a smaller gap between her and the quarry, and as the dog felt the euphoria of the chase, she pulled her forelegs up and sprung onto the rabbit, clenching her jaws around its furry neck, killing it quickly. Fellyn stood still, panting and watching the place behind the trees where Luca had gone, she dared not move in case the rabbit turned back towards her. As she waited she smelled the air, dusk was coming, she saw Luca trot onto their path and come bounding back to her, rabbit in her large jaws, gently held so as not to damage the meat. Fellyn smiled, they would eat well tonight! They walked, side-by-side back to the little bundle of baby that lay close by in thick grass near the stream. As always during a hunt, Fellyn worried about the baby, but she knew the forests, and no predators had been spotted, she knew well that the animals would not trouble the hunting group, they never bothered humans. The two ran back to their little hideaway, the woman chasing the dog, a moment of serenity and happiness in a troubling time. They reached the bushes and Fellyn laid the rabbit at the water's edge, pushed the tall grass apart to reveal the baby, kicking quietly in her blankets, sucking her tiny pink fingers. Fellyn smiled at the angelic face and let the grass fall back into place, turning to the dog who stood in the shallow water, panting. "Wait here, Luca."

Fellyn walked back into the thicker trees and stopped here and there to find branches and twigs for a fire, and walked back to the bushes when she carried an armful. She stopped to touch the trees, feeling the sap, or rubbing the bark. She breathed in the misty air and smelled the natural beauty of the woods around her. It was a stunning place, as she breathed in the warm air she could feel the magic reach her heart, felt it travel up her spine and shivered. As she reached the bushes she could hear that Etana was unsettled, picking the infant up, she felt the material wrapped around the baby and pulled out the pin keeping it secure. She took the soiled sheet to the water and filled up her wineskin; she rinsed the sheet over a muddy patch of grass, washed it in the collected water and laid the sheet out to dry. Fellyn made a fire quickly, she had become good at this despite only doing it once every four to five days, she had not wanted to give away their location in case Jared was close. It was difficult to know how far from the village they had actually travelled and Fellyn wanted to be careful. When she had lit the fire, she moved away to prepare the rabbit while the fire warmed right through.

Many years before...

Tehya shifted the chair closer to the fire and sniffed her broth, sipped it then placed it upon the table to her right. Sat on the floor were three dogs, a cat and a small girl of about ten, so Tehya had guessed. The old woman watched the flames dancing in the girl's eyes and saw the tender movements of her small hands over the largest dog's rump. She was massaging his hind legs, gently moving her fingers in circles and whispering to him, reassuring the animal. Tehya had never seen a young child with such attentiveness and devotion towards animals, such ability, willingness to learn new ways of working, and since the girl had arrived a few weeks back; Tehya had too much business from the villagers and more animals and food than she had ever seen before. Fellyn was a very talented child, and more intelligent than the other children in the village, despite having been clearly neglected and wandering alone in the forests and mountains before resting in Tebel. It was a privilege to be raising her as a woman who had never been allowed to bear children. She remembered the old verses that said women who were not blessed to bear children would raise orphans for the Lord. Yes, she was raising an orphan and was more blessed than she knew!

As Fellyn stopped stroking the dog, she looked up into the face of a woman who had shown her more kindness than she had expected, and despite her memory loss, thought that nowhere else had she been allowed this much love.

Present day...

Jared was never sure where he was in the forest, he had a brilliant ability to track and kill animals because he knew how their minds worked, how they attempted escape and how they moved when they did, but he hated the fact that the forest looked the same everywhere. Fellyn was also not as predictable as a pheasant. She would not follow a flight planned instinctively, or leave tracks that pointed exactly to one resting place, she was going somewhere only she knew. Jared had wondered whether to simply travel to Tehya, she was within forest lands but closer to the village than he currently was. He had lost the tracks and felt he was moving in circles, it was frustrating and tiring, he hadn't eaten well for days and he needed a good night's sleep where leaves were not involved. How was Fellyn coping with Etana to care for too? She was a better survivor than he had bargained for.

He sat again and drank from his wineskin, looking around the forest, he saw trees that all looked the same, plants that served no purpose other than to get in his way, and rabbit droppings. This place made his skin itch with rage, it was a wretched place good only for harbouring animals to kill and eat. He finished the water and made a mental note to find the river again. Yes, he thought. Tehya's was exactly where he needed to go, Fellyn would not be able to resist going to the old hag's shanty hut. He set out on the path to his left and wound a slippery slope downwards that would lead back to the village, it was two days walk back to Tebel, but only a day to Tehya, hopefully he would meet Fellyn there, then he could deal with this ridiculous notion that she would dare to leave his house.

Fellyn decided they needed to speed up their journey so she and Luca were running through the deep woods, following no path but the muddy ground in their sight. Fellyn had done this before as a child, she remembered being in the forests in a cold season, eating spring berries to stay alive and battling her weary brain to stay awake and overcome the cold that she felt deep in her bones. She had been running then too, but from what she still did not know. The heat of sweat steamed from her young body, her hair was coming loose from the ribbon that tied it, and she could feel the material holding Etana to her chest bouncing against her hips. She had to be gentle so as not to shake Etana too much, but the baby didn't seem to mind the movements, in fact she was mesmerised by the trees, the light and the sounds around her. Fellyn was blessed to have a very calm daughter, more interested in taking in everything around her than making any kind of a fuss.

Luca was clearly enjoying herself, tail flying around like a propeller she bounced with ease through the cluttered forest, dodging the old stumps and fallen branches that littered the floor, but she used these as a training course, where Fellyn avoided them when possible. The small family had been on the run for around a week, it was starting to show in Fellyn's body, thinner and less humble than before. Her muscles were defined and her hair a little unruly, she hadn't a comb with them but her fingers had made do. Fellyn began to slow down, gradually coming to a slow walk, Luca returned to her mistress' side and looked up for direction. Fellyn was calmer than she had felt in months, despite her feeling of being hunted, and the constant fear of coming across Jared, she knew that he lacked directional skills, and would not have thought to bring a compass or the advice of any person back at the village. He was stubborn and would try to find them on his own, she knew it. It was that stubbornness which had been so attractive when she had first met him. She recalled the days they had spent in the shallow trees surrounding his mother's farm, Tehya had asked Jared to teach the young seventeen year old how to use a bow and arrow. Fellyn had found his body appealing, his eyes full of intrigue and his mind impenetrable. She had liked that about him. But it was exactly these qualities which were more frightening now, his well toned body was dangerous, his eyes were cold and his mind lacking in conscience. He did not seem to regret hurting her, and if he spoke about his actions, his lies shone through his face. Jared had been a different boy to the man he now was, charming and quiet into convincing and authoritarian. Not the man his father had raised him to be.

Fellyn stopped herself, she was thinking about Jared and it was making her fear their circumstances when she had previously been allowing herself some enjoyment of life. She realised she hadn't been praying recently and shrugged it off, prayer was for those who had gifts to give thanks for, how could she ask for more when she could think of nothing but Etana and Luca to be grateful for in return?

As she walked and wondered how it had happened that her burning passion for her faith had dimmed to a glimpse of light, she saw up ahead a wall. As she moved closer she saw that it was crumbling and riddled with weeds, beetles scurried over its broken surface and made homes in the cracks. She had seen this wall before. It ran for miles in a curve that went on into the horizon the family had been chasing, coming to rest at a large fortress buried in the treetops, invisible to those further than a stone's throw away. Surely this place would be recognisable? Fellyn looked at the ancient building, and despite the concerns that were obvious, here was the perfect place to make camp for a few days while she thought over the plan to reach the mountains. The small group walked onwards, following the wall, stopping here and there to marvel at the structure, and to wonder just how long the bulwark had been standing.

Chapter 2 – Foraging

He looked at his own fist, balled up tightly and split across his middle knuckle, slightly confused, he looked down at where Fellyn lay bleeding slightly from her nose. She was unconscious. Panic flooded his adrenaline fuelled blood and he knelt down to her tender pregnant frame, touching her as gently as he could as if that could balance out the force he had used before. He didn't remember losing his temper, but he did remember the taste of the ale bitter on his tongue, he remembered seeing Rhia on his way home and wanting to touch her but simply tilting his head at her instead, he remembered kissing Fellyn...and then this.

Jared's eyes snapped back into focus as a twig broke nearby, he frowned and his lip pulled back into a sort of snarl as he trod carefully, moving toward the noise. He was close to the thick bushes when a fat pigeon fluttered out in front of him, he cursed the fact that he had not brought a bow and quiver of arrows and carried on through the thick trees.

Fellyn stroked her hand along the old castle wall, feeling the cracks in the strong stones and touching tips of weeds which had wriggled their way into the tiniest of holes and poked out desperate for sunlight.

Fellyn had been heading North of Tebel, following no set path but weaving her own way through the forest so that it was not easy to track her, but she had no plan for her future course. The only thing that crossed her mind about her journey was her memory of the mountains and had always assumed that was where she came from, she had set off in their direction as if unthinkingly returning to them. The castle wall was running East though, totally the wrong direction and dangerous since that would mean the Castle stood near to Cabaro and possibly somewhere she would be easily found. Fellyn looked over at Luca, who was chewing grass, and at Etana who was in her carrying cloth staring wide-eyed at the wall, Fellyn was not sure what they should do here, she was intensely curious about this castle which she had never seen and more so that she could not understand how she had missed it before. They needed to carry on course fast though, if she were to make it over the mountains before winter set in and made it impossible to do so. She had a very thick cloak on, one that she had sewn with hides and furs long ago when she and Jared had been courting, they had hunted the animals together and feasted on their meat before Fellyn had sewn them into a cloak so fine and thick it would keep her protected in a blizzard, she was glad of this now. Fellyn wore a long sleeved white blouse made of wool from some local sheep, it was thick and cosy and she was glad to have been feeling a chill on the night of the fire now since it meant she was dressed warmly. She had thick woollen coverings on her delicate feet under her boots too, her feet tended to run cold as ice so she was always dressed well even in summer. Her long green skirts had been long enough to flow to the ground, but since she had sewn them, they were much easier to move in if not the slightest bit lady-like. Fellyn was blessed to have the warm bundle of baby strapped to her chest as usual, Etana was cosy in her own woollen robe and snuggled tight in her carrying cloth, both mother and child shared their heat. All of this would make no difference if they were exposed when the snows came, their faces and hands uncovered, it would be dangerous to try to pass through the mountains as they were, so she was wary of wasting time. Fellyn looked overhead and saw thick storm clouds rolling in towards them fast, a rain storm would be awful for Etana so she decided to allow herself a couple of days to explore the castle while keeping safely out

21

of the storms. Quickly and carefully she began moving along the great wall, towards the castle set deep in the thickest trees, Luca quick on her heels.

Fellyn was nearing the castle when she stopped their movements, deciding to carry food and drink with them into the castle grounds, for the place was so large that manoeuvring out to search for food after finding a resting spot could take a long time, which she could not waste with Etana strapped to her body. They sat in the shade of an old tree, bearing a fruit whose name Fellyn did not know, it was oval, with waxy purple skin and delicate watery flesh, it was slightly tart but refreshing to eat, this would be good for Etana to taste. Fellyn would wait though, to check that it did not disagree with her own body first. Fellyn filled up the space in their carry pack with the fruit and a few figs they had found recently. She had laid Etana on her cloak to enjoy the fresh air on her little body, and spent some time finding more berries and some twigs and small branches to take with them. She had never asked Luca to carry anything before, but decided that it was worth seeing if the animal would take well to having items strapped to her body, so Fellyn used the ribbon from her hair to securely tie the branches together and then looped the material around the dog's back. Luca sniffed the packaged wood and stood waiting for instruction, all seemed well. After Fellyn had gathered enough to get on with, she strapped Etana to her chest once again and moved towards the castle that stood proudly in their path.

As Fellyn approached the main gate through which they would need to go, she realised that entering the building would be difficult, but she could see rain clouds closing in and knew that her best bet for finding shelter from the rain was in that building. She paced around the gatehouse, trying to see some way, any way to enter the stronghold, but it was impenetrable. Feeling impatient and frustrated at her stupidity for thinking it would be open for access; she removed Etana and laid her in some soft grass in a corner of the wall. "Luca, wait with Etana" She let out her anguish in her voice. She walked up to the large metal gate facing her and assumed that this would most likely be the best way, she could hardly scale the high wall.

Fellyn braced her feet against the soft fallen leaves on the floor and pushed the metal with all the strength she could muster; she switched positions so that her shoulder was against the metal too and marvelled that it had not even creaked under her strain. She moved away, judged the gate again and ran at it, propelling herself using the strength of the floor to lift her, she felt the ground give as she jumped but caught in the downward motion of her own movement she hardly left the floor at all when it disappeared from beneath her feet and she fell into a chasm too deep and dark to understand. Her head was spinning and her ears ringing from the fall, she had knocked her head on the cold floor beneath her. Confused, she felt like the ground under her was not safe and raised her body to her hands and knees to look at it. The hole was too deep to really see much other than the gate directly above them, she panicked. Fear and trepidation entered her as she thought of Etana, lying in the cold grass above her. Nightfall was setting in and as she rubbed her hands against the walls surrounding her in this large hole, she looked at the sheer muddy face of the wall and attempted to climb. Trying for a long time, she could not even reach higher than her own height and a half, Fellyn stood and shouted for Luca, but the dog did not appear at the hole. She had told Luca to stay with Etana, but it seemed odd that she wasn't so much as checking the hole.

All manner of frightening thoughts entered Fellyn's mind, that this was a trap, that she was dead, in Hell or waiting for judgement or maybe that she had simply fallen asleep. No, this was real enough; the pain in her head and the bruises on her legs were proof of that. She had to find her way out, Etana would be alright for a while with Luca, but it was terrifying to think of leaving hearing range of the baby, despite being powerless even if Etana had cried. Fellyn looked around the hole again and saw a wall facing her, a wall which seemed to hold this chasm together, which had obviously been part of some kind of underground network of chambers as it was built with the same bricks that were above her. She pushed at the wall, and remembering how that had gone before, she touched the bricks, determined to find a soft spot to push through, she could see cracking in the patchy light that shone down from above. The largest crack seemed to run down to below floor level, so she used her bruised hands to pull at the dirt and rubble around the place where the wall met the ground. She pulled and dug for what seemed forever, feeling her hands blister and her nails cracking she stopped for breath and examined her fingers, blood ran from an open cut on her ring finger, still holding her wedding band. This was what she deserved for allowing Jared to hurt her and especially Etana, she relished the pain that wound its way around her body, she drank it in and accepted it as her dues. She threw herself once more into removing the rubble, seeing nothing but the same view of the wall, nothing was changing. She felt cold hard metal under her fingers in the dusty earth beneath her feet, and pulling at the ground she saw a pole, she grabbed at it and a handle appeared, with more tugging and digging she removed an old rusted shovel. Caked in grime and dirt, this shovel was a blessing. Saving her hands from further damage she began to hack at the wall using the tool, she pulled at the rubble, moving it from the spot she had fallen to, she was so tired. She stopped to listen for Etana, several hours may have gone by and she had neither seen nor heard anything from above. Shouting once again and getting no response, she screamed up to whoever might hear her

"What am I doing? What now? Please, I need a miracle I cannot move this myself!" she felt anger burning in her throat, she began to sob. Deep racking sobs pulsed through her exhausted body, pushing out the fear that had been dwelling in her heart, releasing the panic she had been feeling for weeks.

Pick up your shovel

"What?" Fellyn sniffed her tears back, she was sure she had heard a voice, so audible and so clear that she was stunned into silence. She waited, daring it to speak again, but the glimmer of hope that had flared inside her was beginning to dwindle when she heard it again.

24

Pick up your shovel and dig

But I can't. Thought Fellyn, despair coursing through her.

You can do all things, for I am your strength. Dig.

Fellyn held the shovel in her hand and stared around her, trying to decide if dehydration or insanity were becoming her companions. She prayed for the strength of an ox, and began to dig at the rubble, finding a new wind she had not foreseen she pushed her body harder and harder, digging at the only exit she could possibly use and as she felt her heart fill with strength and power she saw a hole in the wall open where the rubble used to be. It was enough. Fellyn crawled into the hole, squeezed her shoulders and hips through the wall, wincing as rough stone ran along her tender breasts and stomach, wriggling her legs through and falling to the floor she pushed herself up out of the other side, hoping for some kind of light with which to find her way. All she could see was the darkness of insecurity and fear clouding her mind. She had managed to dig out into the unknown.

It seemed ridiculous that she had put so much effort into breaking into the wall ahead of her, which may not lead to any kind of an exit, in the hope that it was a way to get to Etana. Fellyn pulled her legs free from the bricks around the wall and ran her hands over her skin to check for injuries. She could feel cuts that were stinging and lumps rising on her knees, but she seemed fine otherwise. If only she could see.

Determined to carry on, and not wanting to lose the drive she had found in her heart, she felt around in the darkness, trying to make her eyes find something in the nothingness that surrounded her. She found a wall adjoining the one she had come through so she slowly crept forwards, one hand on the wall, one outstretched in front of her. Tentatively she moved on by placing one foot on the ground and shuffling it around a little to check she was safe and not about to trip or fall. Her heart was pounding with fear and her mind raced with the possibilities of what could be happening to her baby.

She glimpsed a tiny light, tinged blue in the centre and moving further away, was she imagining the light? Fellyn blinked and tried to focus her eyes; she did not want to place all her trust in the light for it may well have been her own mind playing tricks on her. But she felt she had no other choice than to follow the light to see where it led. She moved a little faster, still checking the unseen floor with her feet, she could feel her other senses heightening with the loss of her vision, and listened for any clue about where she could be.

The light vanished as a voice whispered.

Fellyn froze, she was sure someone had muttered but could neither see not hear anything else.

"Hello? Please, is there someone there?"

"Well of course there's someone here I'm standing right in front of you!" the voice replied. It sounded indignant and clearly not impressed with Fellyn's inability to see anything at all. She could hear it muttering under its breath.

"I…I'm sorry, I can't see you." Fellyn blinked into the black unknown, she couldn't even think what to ask someone she could not see so she settled for asking "who are you?"

"Nephi."

"Are you trapped too? It's just that I fell in to this hole and dug my way in here, I can't see or find a way out…" Fellyn felt her throat catch as she stopped herself from mentioning the precious bundle guarded by Luca outside in the coming storm. Guilt flooded her already broken heart and she bit back the sobs that threatened to overwhelm her.

"You won't find a way out, that's the whole point of having a maze under here." Nephi chuckled. Fellyn turned her head to either side, desperately trying to see something, or to understand why this situation warranted laughter.

"What exactly are you trying to achieve by twitching like that?"

"Well I can't see!" Fellyn said, turning her head side to side in exasperation, she felt like she may as well be alone again for all the help she was getting.

"When you find yourself incapable of sight, it becomes imperative to open your eyes!" Nephi shouted with a laugh. "Why, everyone else can see fine!"

Fellyn could feel her anger burning again, frustrated and cold she let out a cold laugh.

"Please help me find a way out; I need to get back to my daughter!"

Nephi pondered her request and moving towards Fellyn, stared into the woman's eyes and felt her desperation.

"Well finally, I get to hear your real reason for panic." Nephi concentrated, lit up his long fingers with a blue tinged hue and moved them towards Fellyn.

"Are you….is your hand doing that" she asked, blinking in the light that was so welcome but made her eyes water from being in the dark so long.

Nephi stood, smiling into her grubby face, he leaned in closer to her and whispered teasingly "Don't tell anyone about this, hm?"

Fellyn stood and took in as much of her surroundings as she could, and looked again at Nephi, he seemed to shimmer in the blue light, never quite the same colour or size twice. He was fairly tall, lithe and graceful with long legs and a long face, his strong jaw was prominent and his eyes were very large. They seemed to burn like embers, the reddish brown moving and flickering as if they housed a merrily burning fire inside them. She could barely see his hands for the bright light that shone from his fingertips, yet she could tell they were long too. He didn't seem to be touching the floor, which was marbled and dirty, rather he skimmed the surface, Fellyn pondered this as she looked at him. "What are you?"

"I am older than this castle and made of more than mere body." He answered, Fellyn got the feeling this wasn't a welcome discussion, so quietened, following his footsteps as he slowly and gracefully moved along the dank corridor.

Tehya had talked of Elvin people before with high regard, Fellyn wished she has asked more questions, feeling she could be looking at one now, but Tehya's idea of normal talk was not the same as the others in Tebel so Fellyn had learned to differentiate the two and had stopped asking.

Fellyn realised that Nephi had been talking the whole time she was thinking about Tehya, and focused on the question she had to ask him. "So…are you an elf?"

Nephi merely turned to her, smiled and went silent.

28

It occurred to Fellyn that despite being completely panicked about moving deeper underground and further from Etana, and feeling her heart want to burst out of her chest or shake Nephi to make him help, he seemed more cooperative when she was calm with him. So she planned instead to speak gently to him and ask more specific questions. She reached out to touch his muscular shoulder, and without seeing her, he flinched before she could make contact with his iridescent skin, he spun on the spot and stared into her eyes. He was mesmerizing. His eyes blazed a wildness and his brows furrowed, "Why do you question where I take you, when there is only one direction in which to travel?" he said plainly, angrily even.

"I...I just need to get out, please" she begged, she wrapped her arms around her own shoulders, his eyes were boring into her, seeking out her weaknesses she felt, she closed up around herself and looked at her feet, longing for him to look away and not see her for all her brokenness.

He released a small sigh, and whispered gently, as if to a startled bird "Just, please, follow me, I know the way you need to go."

Without thinking of any reason not to, and without wondering about his calmness, she raised her chin and followed him further, deeper under the castle grounds because she had no other choice but to let her guard down for once and trust this strange man.

Chapter 3 – Garden of Nephi

Fellyn was watching the tall figure of Nephi, they had been walking for what seemed hours, winding and turning the labyrinthine paths of the castle's underground tunnel. Here and there along the path, Fellyn would see shapes carved intricately into the wall, little images of knights and dragons, battle shields and flags and sometimes odd symbols which meant nothing to her. Nephi stopped short, Fellyn, who had not been concentrating on his passage but on the walls stopped just short of walking into the tall figure. Nephi turned and smiled at the tired young woman, "you need to rest." He said.

Fellyn rather thought he was stating the obvious and snorted to herself, she had no intention of stopping even to catch her breath, with her daughter exposed to the elements with only Luca for protection, and with no access to food, Fellyn knew it wouldn't take long for Etana to cry out and attract predators…or people. A shiver shot down her spine at the thought of Jared finding the little baby before she did, of him returning to the village with the girl and telling some story of her being lost in the castle, of how the young mother had abandoned Etana. Fellyn's heart began pounding again and she found herself racing through all the ways she would hurt whoever took her baby from Luca's side.

Feeling a shift in the emotion in the dark tunnel, Nephi stood and stared into Fellyn's eyes which were far away in her own fears. He could see into her troubled soul and understood how far she had yet to go.

30

"Come, Fellyn, you'll need rest soon" he said and without touching her, he gestured her to follow again.

The pair walked not a hundred more yards before he came to a brick arch in the wall; it was closed in with stone of another kind. Fellyn raised her eyebrows in concern, she wanted so much to ask what it was, why it was closed and why Nephi was even down here in the first place. She wanted to know why this place had tunnels under it, and why she had fallen into it, and how exactly Nephi planned to get out. She needed to know what made his skin shimmer like light reflecting off of the surface of water, and why his eyes were like pools of fire. But she had no words that weren't fuelled by panic, and no way to word her curiosity so she stopped and watched him. Nephi's eyes were closed now, his translucent eyelids moving and twitching, showing her that his eyes were flickering though shut. Just when she felt the need to prod him in case he was sleeping, his eyes opened and so did the wall. The brick simply wasn't there anymore. Fellyn was blinded by bright sunlight, the hottest and most beautiful of skies she had seen in weeks. Her eyes, so accustomed to the dark tunnels were useless in the light and she blinked like a mole in daylight, waiting for her brain to catch up with her surroundings. When the spots in her vision faded, and the day became clear, she looked all around; there were rows and rows of plants and bushes. Trees in full blossom though it was out of season for that, reeds sprouting from the most clear water pool she had ever seen. The smell was phenomenal, all of the scents of the blooms around her complimented each other, herb and flower and vegetation alike all blended into an aroma she felt she already knew. Somehow, she felt this was her home and yet she knew it never had been. Amazed, she bent to study the most beautiful blue flowers before her feet, stunning, shaped like little bells and delicately balanced on their spindly stems, she stretched a hand to touch one and could practically hear the chiming they made, just like a bell; but in the most inaudible of little rings. All fear had vanished from her, she was stunned by the sheer beauty of the garden and the comfort all around her. After a while of walking and studying this splendid place, it dawned on her that when she had fallen into the pit, she had left Etana and Luca with a brewing storm overhead in the waiting dusk at

31

dimming light. She had not thought it had been a whole night though she knew it had been a rather long time. Panic, again rose inside of her and she began to look for a way out, when her eyes met Nephi's she began to calm a little.

"Nephi…I need to get to her, my baby, please, how do I get out, please…" she could hear the desperation in her voice and she resented herself for it. Nephi came forwards, walking, or gliding was probably a more accurate term, towards her. He held out a hand, a hand such a delicate shade of pale blue shimmering like the water, and when she reached out her own she felt it was too delicate to touch, so she simply held it outstretched, neither one touching the other. He led her to the clear pool, held up a robe that had sat unnoticed beside it, a robe of velvet the exact colour of the bluebells she had adored, trimmed in exquisite silk and adorned with delicate silver thread crisscrossing the chest. He gestured to the pool and said "bathe here, Fellyn, its safe here." Leaving her there with the robe and the pool, Nephi walked from the garden, through the same arch they had come from and into the darkness.

Fellyn looked around the garden, she was very self-conscious in that open space, feeling exposed and on show despite there being nobody else around, she stripped down to her undergarments and slid into the pool. It was cool but not cold, refreshing, like it was running from a deep spring underground. She paddled over to the rushes and washed herself hidden behind the lovely reeds, she allowed herself a real soak in the water, and washed all the grime of the tunnel from her raw hands, from her nail beds and the lines on her face. Fellyn allowed herself to relax in the water for a moment, drinking in the feeling of contentment, and when she brought her hands up from the water to run them through her hair she turned them over in disbelief. Her hands were perfect, no cuts or grazes from digging at the stones…as if she had washed the wounds away along with the dirt.

Mesmerised and clean, she rose from the water and tentatively used her own clothes to pat herself dry and slipped her undergarments and stockings back on. She slipped the bluebell robe over her head and looked down, it fit her well and accentuated her young body, she turned and knelt down to wash her clothes in the water, hanging them on the side of a small wall to dry. She turned around, and moving her damp hair from her face she saw Nephi standing a few yards away, watching her curiously. Fellyn blushed a deep crimson, wondering how long he had stood there, and catching herself for being stupid enough to forget where she was. He walked towards her and offered his hand, in it, he held out a loaf of bread, a flat bread which seemed to be made with seeds and oats for she could see them in the rough doughy surface. She took the bread gently, thanked him for the kindness, and wondering how he had gotten the bread, she bit into it and found herself needing to sit. The bread was the most delicious she had ever tasted, rich and yet mild in flavour, it had subtle tones of flavour including a meat and vegetable combination which she found it hard to explain. At home, her bread tasted merely of the yeast and salt needed to give it some appeal and rise. This bread filled her like no meal had ever done, quenched all her hunger and she could feel the ripple of goodness spread inside her.

She stared up into Nephi's handsome face, her eyes questioning everything about him and this strange place and his strange food. Nephi's smile was answer enough, he himself was like nothing she had ever seen or known, so why was she so questioning of this gift of bread. Heavenly, she told herself. This place feels heavenly. Wondering if she were dreaming, she realised she had finished the bread, and Nephi was holding out to her a goblet of pewter, she took it and inside saw a deep crimson wine. Wincing a little at the stench of alcohol in the cup, it reminded her of a raised fist and an angry voice inside her bitter memories. She took a sip, but again, tasted something exquisite, the like of which she had never known. Whatever vines were growing the crop to make this wine must have been planted by the hands of God himself for the taste they gave! She drank deeply of the cup, and patting her mouth dry, handed the cup back to Nephi. He avoided her fingers again when receiving the cup, and he set it onto the low wall which she now noticed was running across the garden, and aside from the small gap for the path, was separating the garden blooms from a completely unsown patch of soil.

"Will you not eat?" Fellyn asked, worried that she had cleared out his meal. Nephi chuckled a little.

"I do not need to eat of the bread and drink the wine as you do, for I do not have the same human needs as you." Fellyn frowned at him, confused. Before she could question him further, he clapped his hands together.

Nephi, smiling at the newly cleaned woman in front of him, looked more amused than he had since Fellyn had met him, she smiled back, unable to help herself and as he turned and walked away, she felt comfortable to simply follow in step behind him and trust him to take her somewhere closer to her darling daughter. A peaceful serenity was flowing in her, perhaps from the heavenly drink she had taken, but she was much more calm and happy with everything facing her. When she realised Nephi had taken her into a room, she had no idea what direction they might have gone to get there, he had led her to a small room at the top of a flight of stairs, and in the room she saw a large four poster bed draped with rich furs and velvet sheets. Nephi held the door open to her, and she walked into the room, spinning around her to see the sheer beauty in the room despite the slightly crumbled walls, and the dank unkempt look of the window which was caked in grime from what must be centuries of neglect. Nephi watched her walk to the window, try to wipe it clear and give up, then cross the room and sit on the bed, she stroked the sheets with her beautiful long fingers, and smiled up at him. He smiled back and sat in a small wooden chair near the door. There they sat for a while, until Nephi spoke "What made you come to the castle, Fellyn?"

She blinked at him, she realised she had never actually told him her name.

"I...needed somewhere to hide from the storm, to rest with my daughter and dog...I'm sorry if you thought me trespassing I didn't know anyone was still here."

Nephi's face changed slightly, his fiery eyes burned brighter, "no, Fellyn, I didn't mean the weather and the baby; I know Etana is safe and well and unharmed by the storm. I meant why are you out in the forest so alone?"

Fellyn's face fell at the sound of her precious daughter's name, how did he know that too? Where was her daughter and why did he sound so sure that she was fine? Strangely, Fellyn still didn't feel threatened by him but she was still intensely worried about her baby girl and could feel her breasts swelling with the milk she needed to feed Etana. Her mind was weak with a strange sensation as a fogginess clouded her thoughts and pushed her towards exhaustion.

Nephi leaned forward, elbows on his knees "now, Fellyn, please don't think me rude. You are safe here, I came to you with a message,"

Baffled, she looked at his honest face and fiery eyes, his skin which seemed to move even as she stared at his hands, this man she knew nothing about, who had found her in the impossible pitch-black tunnel system. She pondered how he had known she was there, and how he could possibly have a message, and from whom? Fellyn's heart beat faster, waiting for his message. "What message?" she croaked, dangerously close to losing her temper at her situation.

"I came simply to tell you...you are here to receive truth about who you are."

Her heart fell...she had no idea who she was or where she belonged, so what did this strange man know of her, and just as she intended to protest what he had said, she felt herself drift into sleep, unaware that she was even falling in the first place.

Rhia stood in the village square, it was ringed with lovely flowers which had been planted in old feeding troughs and barrels that were too damaged to hold water for animals. In one arm she held a small basket of baked bread from her neighbour and in the other she held a pail of water from the stream which flowed through the centre of the village. They were lucky here for the water was clean and untainted, a simple wooden bridge lay over the stream, dividing the village into two halves, on one side lived the less wealthy of the village and on the other were those whose living was paid in wages from the High council or the Guard. Rhia was the wife of a Councillor, their chief, Cassius. She had met him in Cabaro where she had been raised, and he had brought her bouquets of flowers all the way from the Moranye Mountains, where Varose lay in the clouds of the tallest peak. He brought her chickens to feed her family, and beautiful gifts of exquisite cloth and occasionally perfumes. Rhia had not really felt anything towards Cassius, he was charming enough, sure, but he was not the most attractive of men, nor had he any real idea of conversation to please a woman, he simply paid for her attention. It had been Rhia's mother that had decided he would be a good husband; Rhia was raised in a modest household of farmers, one of eleven children and the oldest daughter after three older brothers. She was used to going without, or making do and getting on, she had not been expecting nor comfortable with Cassius' extravagant advances but her mother was smitten with the man, and her dear father, God rest his soul, had seen the potential of a good life for his daughter in a wealthy enough man. So she had married Cass for his money, shamefully, and spent her days raising their two boys with no passion for the man in her bed but for the love she felt which was more of a caring than a desire.

Rhia missed her farming roots, she missed her dear father who had died suddenly as so many men did in Xandia, and left her mother with seven children still at home. She dearly missed their grubby faces and the long days running the homestead or at the market selling cheese and eggs. Rhia never saw her family any more, even though Cassius went to Cabaro regularly, he never allowed her to go there and visit, he instead went and gave money to her mother to help her. Rhia was thankful enough for her comfortable life and for her two boys, but she longed for excitement and passion.

As Rhia rounded a corner to get back to their house on the wealthier side of Tebel, she heard Iris Brown talking loudly to a group of other women, she went over to them to say hello and to see what they were gossiping about.

"Burned for ages it did, right up like it was planned!"

"No! What abou' the girl and that wee babe?"

"Must have been in it when it went up, t'were late in the evening! No-one's seen hide nor hair of them...scuse my bluntness!"

"Old Obadiah says he saw them running through the orchards, d'yu think she got out alright?"

"Mark my words, whatever's hauntin' that girl aint stopping yet!"

"Don't be daft, Iris, she's just unlucky see, some folks are just accident prone, maybe she lit the fire bad."

Rhia was curious, she hadn't seen any fire nor smoke at all, but living on the other side of the bridge meant she was often the last to hear the local news. "Good morning Iris, Sylvie...Magi, why, what has happened to have you all so flustered?" Rhia teased gently.

"The Kellack girl, caught in a fire, see, whole house burned before the rain came and the men had it put out. Didn' you know?" Iris said, clearly enjoying being the messenger.

"No...I didn't...did you say she got out?" Rhia asked, breathy with concern for Jared and his little wife and baby.

"Obe seems to think they did, by you know Obe...he might be rememberin' seeing them last Sabbath in the Orchard and confused in his drinkin'!" Magi said with a giggle, Rhia frowned at her, this was hardly a funny topic of conversation since nobody seemed sure whether Fellyn and Etana had gotten out safely.

"Has nobody checked the house for bodies?" Rhia asked the women, quietly as if already in reverence for the dead.

"They've been clearing the rubble, darlin'." Said Sylvie kindly. "Jared hasn't been home yet if that's what you're wonderin', I don' think he knows what 'appened." Sylvie touched Rhia's arm gently, which made Rhia pull hers away as if the allegation that she cared more for Jared than for the fate of Fellyn and her baby had bruised her, when really it had been right on the money. Ashamed of this, Rhia muttered a thanks and goodbye to the ladies and moved back the way of the Kellack house, it was set in thick trees at the very end of the long village since they had been the most recent of villagers to build a home. She heaved the bread basket more comfortably on her hip and shifted the pail slightly, and sped up her pace. As she rounded a couple of saplings to get nearer the house, she could smell the smoky breeze and hear men chatting as they sifted through burned rubble, looking for bodies of people that were a part of the small community. The sight of the charred ruins made her stomach turn, the thought of little Etana caught in such a terrible blaze chilled her heart and sent her into a worry, but also for Jared, who could well be very much alone from now on. This last thought didn't bother her as much as it should have, and she mentally gave herself a telling off. Rhia shook her pretty hair at the terrible sight, she would need to tell Cassius and they could set about to help the family...or what was left of it.

Chapter 4 – Jared's Path

Jared stood in front of Tehya's hut, the roses creeping in vines up the left side of the house, the guttering she had attached was held in place with twine which creaked and groaned in the wind, leading down to a large container gathering the rain which was coming down steadily now. Jared glanced at the herb garden, Tehya's skilled hands could raise and grow anything but the herb garden was full of weeds and he could see a nest of ants making their way up the growing pea plants. Furrowing his brow in concern, he knocked gently on the door of the hut and waited. No answer. He knocked again a couple more times, and seeing no response he began his way around the back along the short path leading to her glade, where she had penned a goat and a few chickens. As he walked around the bend to the glade he saw Tehya there, limping gently as she often did these days and gently rubbing circular motions on the rump of the goat. Jared was glad of the spare milk she sometimes shared with them, but aside from that, her affection towards the animal confused him, it was for milk, then meat and pelt when it died but she treated it like a beloved house guest!

Thinking Tehya could not see him there was a mistake "Hello, Jared. It's been a long time since you've come to visit me." She said, with very little warmth in her voice. He scowled, the old crone had ears like a bat no matter how mad she was.

"No, Tehya, that's true. But my wife seems to have gone off on her own. With the baby and Luca." He felt his anger growling up inside him like an animal, the walking had soothed his ego momentarily but here he felt it awaken and roar. "Since you're her only family I guessed I'd find her here so where is she?" he looked around the small glade, in the little shelter kept standing only for the goat's sake, poked his head under a large bush and stamped his feet when he found nothing but a chicken disgruntled at being bothered. Tehya smiled and tilted her old wizened head. "If you've lost your wife carelessly, what makes it business of mine?" she said

Jared frowned at the crone again, she made his blood boil, this little witch who lived on her own so far from the village, who barely even saw Fellyn these days yet called herself family, she would pay if she had dared help Fellyn run anywhere!

Tehya stopped stroking the goat, picked up the small pail of milk she had gotten from the old girl today, scattered a few small bits of stale bread she had in her pocket for the hens and watched them greedily peck at the grass. Looking up into Jared's face, Tehya saw his troubles and all his shame, knew how he was breaking down his family by giving in to the anger that coursed through his veins, and drowning himself in drink daily to try and forget his pain. If she could nurse a human's mind the way she could heal her animals, she would be rich by now, so she simply sighed and looked at the tall man in front of her. "Jared Kellack, you've been my family since you came here with your bow more times than I'd asked you just to see that girl. She is my daughter, no blood but in here" she gestured over her heart. "That girl is frightened of you and all your anger, if you want someone to blame for her running off then you need to look deep at your marriage." Tehya wasn't done there, but before she could say any more, Jared raged up to her, towering over her head and all the fury he held was pouring from him like smoke from a burning rag.

"TELL me where she is, Tehya, I am the head of that woman, I tell her where to go and when, not her and certainly NOT you!" He was just reigning in his anger, desperate not to hit the frail old woman when she laughed in his face.

40

"No, Jared, under God's eyes she swore obedience, but din' you swear to respect her...?"

Jared turned and stormed from the little clearing, he didn't need the idiocy of some old crone, he knew what he had done and it was what any husband would do to control a flighty wife.

When he reached the narrow path leading back to Tebel, he stood at the small intersection and looked around him. He had lost her trail, come on a fools mission to question Tehya, and ended up no closer to finding her than the night he had left to follow after her. He would go home, and try to find some reason for her leaving.

When he strolled into the higher end of the village through the thinner trees from Tehya's glade, he walked past the three wealthier family huts including the chief's house and then crossed the little bridge to the lower end of the village, past small rows of huts which housed the poorer families in Tebel, he felt uneasy. Something was wrong. The usual hustle and bustle of people working outside, chopping firewood and skinning their dinner were not happening. People were stood in small rings, muttering quietly, or otherwise shutting their doors and bolting them when Jared walked past. He was a popular face in the village, people needed his hunting skills for food, and Fellyn was beloved for her kindness with the fruit she grew, their behaviour ran a tingle of confused anger down his spine but then he looked up from the houses he had been ogling and stopped dead. Right in front of him, down what had been their pretty little path with rose bushes and wild herbs growing was now a scorched wasted frame of his house.

Picking up into a run, he reached his home, where he and his brothers had spent days erecting the beams and frame, packing the earth and dung into the walls and then letting them bake in the sun. The roof he had packed by hand and tied with thick twine. The beautiful door he had made from chopped oak of a stunning tree they had felled themselves for this house. None of it remained. He bent to the ground and touched the ash with his dirty fingers, crumbled a piece of charred wood and wiped the blackened stain on his shirt. Inside the frame, it was a mess of burned, or half salvaged belongings. He could see the headboard of their bed sat on the floor in a pile of rubble that must have been their bed. The cradle made of woven twigs and thick pelts was fine though and it made his heart bleed for his baby girl, somewhere far from his reach. That precious little thing he adored and couldn't wait to teach to walk, and run and eventually hunt. Jared suddenly understood what had made Fellyn run, he stood slowly, and turned to see a small group of villagers staring at him. Rhia, the chief's lovely wife walked slowly up to him, a pail of water and a basket of bread by her feet her, one hand holding that of her little son, Davey. She came and rested her lovely tanned hand on his shoulder, leaned towards him and whispered that they hadn't found bodies, but that old Obadiah swore he saw her running from the flames into the orchard carrying the baby and wearing her thickest cloak.

Jared knew this anyway, it had been Obadiah that had told him what he had seen in the tavern, he had failed to mention the burning house before Jared had had time to run out into the forest after her. He realised he had been quick to assume she had run from her marriage to him, perhaps because he felt guilty for causing her to fear him. Jared nodded mutely and stared into Rhia's green eyes. "Obe told me…I thought….I didn't know." He said. Rhia simply patted his shoulder again, pulling him towards her and Davey. She bent down and handed the bread basket to her young boy and took the water pail in one hand and using the other hand she led Jared back through the village, over the bridge and past the tavern towards her house.

"We've got hot broth at home, come and eat, you must be starving." She said quietly, giving harsh looks to all the folk who were talking under their breath about Jared's home, wife and child.

Reaching their pretty home, Jared wiped his boots on the mat and entered, Davey followed and after putting the basket hastily on the table he rushed over to his little chair by the fire. He smiled up at Jared and pointed to the seat their father usually occupied. Jared felt uneasy, he liked Rhia and her boys, they were eager learners and her boys loved to help him make bows for hunting, they were a little young to learn to shoot yet, but he had shown them how to skin and gut the game and they always sat attentively, learning the tricks of the trade and talking about what they would hunt when they, too, became men. Rhia was...well...Rhia was everything Jared had always expected Fellyn to be. She was beautiful, yes, in a very simple way, and she laughed often, she was always singing when doing her daily jobs and she was kind hearted. She treated Jared like he was man of the house when her husband was away, he hunted for them and took care of the logs for her fire, and in return, she offered him her company, her understanding and her loyalty. He had always thought perhaps if things had been different, if he had met Rhia first then perhaps he would be with her instead. Rhia had come from the main town, had met the chief when he was visiting and he had admired her beauty. They weren't romantic or loving to one another and he was jealous for her, that he wasn't able to offer her what she really deserved in a husband and what he wished he could do for her in the chief's place. But he had never betrayed Fellyn other than to spend more time with Rhia than was really necessary. Fellyn...his broken home re-entered his mind. The ash...the singed cradle and the dead flowers pained him. His heart ached for Fellyn and he wondered what she had done to cause such a raging fire...was she frightened of him? Was that why she ran away?

When Rhia came into the little hut, her arms clutching her woven fire basket full of logs and kindling twigs and kicked the door closed behind her, Jared's mind flittered from his broken home back to Rhia. He watched as she stoked her fire and added another log, Jared saw her struggle with the heavier logs he rose quickly, gently touched her arm and took the log from her hand, she stroked his arm in return, smiled and headed to the stove where she put a pot of water on to boil. The broth was bubbling and when Rhia lifted the lid, the meaty aroma flooded the kitchen, Jared smiled and finishing putting the larger logs in the fire he turned to Rhia and thanked her for her kindness.

"You've no need to thank me…it must be a shock after seeing the house…how are you feeling?" she asked, genuinely concerned about him. It was nice to be cared about for a change.

"I'm fine, Rhia, concerned about the weather and getting another house built but I suppose we will make do at my mother's for a time…" he left the sentence trailing off, realising with a stab again that he had to find Fellyn…and he had to build a new home. It felt too much, he was also a day away from his usual big hunt, he needed to catch more game for the families he usually fed, and for his own store but he wouldn't be likely to manage that now. All of his belongings were probably gone…his bow and arrows were safe along with his knives in the woodshed which stood further back from the house and had been unscathed. But he had no spare clothes nor any home comforts.

Seeing his concern, Rhia put down the broth pan and spoon she held and wrapped his large hand in both of her small warm ones, she looked deep into his eyes and spoke firmly, "we will all help, we can all build a house in a short time, the fallow field behind your woodshed will do, and once the old frame and rubble have been moved, we can plough the area for your crops. I will make sure you have somewhere to stay and we can help you with food. You already do enough for our family…let me repay you this way…please?" her honest eyes and kind heart warmed Jared's weariness. He lowered his voice into a mere whisper.

"Thank you…you are so very kind to me, Rhia." She blushed and heard the door creak, Jared turned to see Rhia's older boy Marcus enter the warm hut with a loaf of bread in one arm, and a pail of water in the other. When Jared looked back to Rhia, she had turned her eyes back to the broth and busied herself with bowls and spoons, the air thick with their unspoken words.

Marcus' eyes fell on Jared and he bounded over excitedly "Jared, you're here! Will you hunt with us tomorrow, can we fish soon, we haven't had fish in such a long time, papa says we can take next Sabbath off and go with you, can we? Please?" the lad was bouncing on his toes and grinning, Rhia sighed and in defence of Jared, knowing how hard he would be working to fix his broken life, she spoke words of disappointment to her little boy.

"Marcus, Jared can't go with you for a while now, his home will need building, and it won't be for you boys to be getting in the way. Can you please go and tell your father than his supper is done?" she smiled encouragingly, a trait Jared admired in her, the ability to make everything worth smiling for.

"Yes mama." Marcus was clearly dejected, but he was a good lad and placing the water on the small family table, he went back out into the village to find his father.

"I will need to hunt soon, for all of us, I don't mind taking your Marcus, he's a good kid and I'm sure he would be able to handle it soon." He said, he spoke quietly, so as not to upset Davey who was sat in his little chair, playing with a wooden box and stones, creating his own little world. Jared envied his innocence.

"No, Jared, you don't need to be taking care of my son when you have so much on your plate as it is." She smiled again, radiant.

"I think of them as practically my own" he said, unthinkingly. "Like family, I mean." He corrected. But her warm smile hadn't altered and she glanced sideways at him sweetly, she wasn't unhappy with him caring for her boys as sons.

Suddenly hit by a wave of guilt and concern for his lost wife, he decided to go and search for her tracks again, knowing it had been a night and day already and his odds were slim.

"I need to find Fellyn…I'll be alright tonight at my mother's Rhia, but thank you for offering your home to me." He took her hand, kissed it gently and walked to the door, little Davey popped up his dark head and waved goodbye, Jared waved back, smiled at Rhia's stunned expression and disappeared out of the door.

"You didn't eat…" Rhia said quietly, looking at the fifth bowl of broth she had laid for him, she tipped it back into the pot for later and slipped the bowl back on to the table, empty.

Jared shook his head in the dwindling light of the evening, what was he doing getting close to Rhia when Fellyn was in the forest somewhere, alone with Etana to care for. He set off straight to the orchard, and followed the path she must have trodden. He scanned the area repeatedly, checking for signs she had left the main track that he might have missed before, but found nothing. He walked in the growing cold, wishing he had brought his thick winter cloak and then realising it would have been burned in the fire. Gritting his teeth, he walked faster, following the tracks until he could no longer see his feet in the darkness. The moon was barely visible through the clouds, giving him very little light to see the path ahead but he carried on following his gut feeling of her direction. As he trod the only path through the woods this way, he felt he was being watched, shivered and brushed it off as tiredness. He hadn't seen the figure silently sweep through the trees behind him, keeping hidden but following his every step.

46

Chapter 5 – Trials and Testing

Fellyn groggily felt herself slipping out of a glorious dream, a garden, such a splendid place. And a man made of something like water. She sat bolt upright and gasped. It hadn't been a dream, Etana was all alone with Luca, outside of the castle and she was inside with Nephi. She couldn't remember getting to this room, and had no reason, that she could remember, for why she slept…nor any idea how long had she slept. She rose quickly, and stumbled, feeling her head foggily she waited for the dizziness to pass and then looked down at her robe, it was the bluebell dress with silver thread that Nephi had given her to wear, it all came back to her in snippets, the pond, the wall around the unplanted patch of soil, the stairs and the room and his message. She opened the door, surprised, she half expected it to be locked. She ran down the stairs as fast as she could, reached a corridor going to either direction so she turned both ways; they looked identical. Choosing on impulse as she had no memory of the way back to the courtyard, she turned left and ran as far as she could, she passed several shut doors and then came to another decision, she chose right this time and followed the corridor, trying not to get herself lost. Deciding to find a door to try, she retraced her steps and the first door she came to led to stairs heading downwards. Figuring the garden to be on a lower level, she followed the stairs and came again to a corridor, this time heading forwards only. Walking now, to catch her breath, she followed the path and came to a slightly damp area of the flagstones. Looking up to the door ahead of her she saw water was coming from underneath it, slowly running outwards nearer her feet. A curious mixture of intrigue and fear surged through her but despite that, she sloshed through the puddle, opened the door and entered.

Inside the room it was cold and clammy, the walls were wet and she shivered as the thought of icy cold water filled her thoughts. She walked slowly, through the wet room, the water level reaching the straps of her boots. Glancing around, confused, she saw a plaque on the wall in brass, Fellyn walked closer, sloshing her boots in the water as she went and saw the words "Water Arena" and puzzled by this, moved towards the door at the end of the sodden corridor.

Pushing open the door she walked into a room with a low ceiling and tight walls. It was a flat room, with carved benches forming a semi circle facing what appeared to be a platform in the centre of the room. On the other side of the platform, from one end of the long room to another, a river of clear water flowed through a grated hole in the wall across to another grate the other end, but the water was overflowing onto the platform and it was causing the water to run across the floor and through the four doors placed equally around the semi circle of chairs. It had the feel of a great place but it reeked with something like mould and neglect and she shuddered at the question that formed in her mind, *what kind of a place is this?*

One chair was raised up in the very centre point of the benches on the semi circle, it was carved in exquisite dark wood and inlaid with carvings so beautiful that Fellyn desired to look closer and touch the mighty chair. Walking slowly to avoid the echo her footsteps had caused, and cautiously working her way through the seating, she stared at the chair and felt a tingle down her spine. The carvings were of the most beautiful angels, raised high on the back of the chair, towering above naked men and women below who were all wrapped in a tangle of limbs, raging with lust and brutal fighting. She looked again at the angels, they were reaching their hands towards the humans below them, with tragic longing on their perfect carved faces. One face struck a chord with her, it looked like Nephi…she reached out her hand to stroke his face and she remembered how he avoided her touch. When her fingers made contact with the face of the carved angel, she heard a loud noise like the unlocking of a door and turned in fright to see the

water flowing and surging over the river's stone bank, she saw a crack across the grate going into the wall above it and realised it was pulsing water out at a staggering rate. Water was inching closer to her, flowing out in ripples of the semi circle platform and coursing over the seating. As it closed in all around her, trapped in the middle of the seating and flowing around her on all sides, she panicked and turned to her left and tried to run. The water level was rising and the flat design of the room was moving it fast towards her, *so much water* she thought to herself. Splashing through the ankle high water she reached a door on the far left, opposite where she had entered, the door refused to move, the water was rising past her boots and filling them with a chilling flood. The icy feel against her toes plunged her deep into her memories.

She was walking through the mountain valley clutching on to an arm she felt was her only hope, her hands were bound with rope and her companion was tied too. Their feet were bound with one long piece of rope tied around both feet, so they had only enough length to shuffle rather than walk. There were dark figures walking in front and behind them, she could feel hot breath on her uncovered neck, driving snow blew into their faces, biting at Fellyn's nose and ears, she could no longer feel her hands or feet and was beginning to feel sleepy in the freezing force of snow. Something hard and sharp prodded her in the back and fear surged through her body

"Keep moving, girl!" A man's voice bellowed in her ear.

She huddled closer to the girl at her side, smaller than she was and stunningly beautiful, her blue-grey eyes with their streak of black staining the iris were half closed with exhaustion and her hands were red raw from the freezing cold. Red welts ringed her hands and feet too where the rope was rubbing and burning her delicate skin and her breathing was shallow and frail. Fellyn felt the fear of loss circling in her mind and she took her companion's hands in her own bound ones, moving awkwardly for the rope around them and the stiffness in her fingers, she heard a sigh from beside her and could feel the slight relief from the girl's pretty face. "Thank you, sister" she mouthed into the cold air.

"We'll camp here, they won't last long. We need them alive." A voice as cold as the driving snow said, and Fellyn felt herself being prodded right, towards an open cave entrance on the side of the mountain wall. They moved into the darkness,

49

feeling relief as they were sheltered from the driving snow. The hand pushed them towards the very back wall, quite a way into the cave and they were shoved to sitting on a pile of cold stone. Fellyn unwrapped her hands from her sister's and saw they were tinged with blue at the tips of her fingers, she bent her head close to them and put them in her mouth, desperate to warm them and keep the cold from robbing her sweet baby sister of her hands. The warmth in Fellyn's mouth spread to the frozen hands and she could feel them gradually return to a less terrifying temperature, the pain of warmth was bitter sweet to the young girl and she started losing consciousness on Fellyn's shoulder. Bound and awkward, there was no easy way to hold her dear sister so she settled herself into a rock crevice and let the girl fall asleep on her shoulder.

Fellyn blinked at her predicament, where had the memory come from, so real and so painful? She felt a surge of pain stab at her heart and the overwhelming grief of the little girl flooded her. She shook her head to clear her mind and looked down, water was reaching her knees and the door refused to budge, so while being dragged down by the weight of her water logged robe, she pushed her way through the flood and came to the next door. Tugging hard at the ring handle and pulling as hard as she could, she knew there was no way to move it. Rust or time perhaps seemed to have closed it tight and with the tugging at her body that the water created, she hadn't the momentum to pull any harder so she pushed away again to move to another door. Reaching the third she decided to return to the furthest, knowing it must work because it was the one through which she had come. Water was reaching her waist now and she felt herself curse the water-tight room, panicking that she had no way of knowing if there would be any crevice that the water would rush through fast enough to relieve her of the speedy onslaught. She began to swim rather than push through on her feet, awkwardly, she had never been a strong swimmer and she feared the deep waters. Reaching the door she pulled and pulled but nothing moved, the water was stronger and the force was stopping the door from opening.

"HELP....NEPHI...ANYONE, HELP ME!" Fellyn screamed, standing again and feeling the water reach her rib cage, she began to panic. The temperature in the room was dropping, she was confused and too consumed with finding an exit to notice the layer of ice that was spreading along the top of the water. Gradually and slowly working its way towards her and as she turned and saw it creeping her way, a memory flashed, consumed her mind.

The men were sat around a small fire, laughing and joking among themselves, there were seven of them all and they were large; built for fighting. The one with his back to the girls had a crossbow slung across his shoulder and a dagger at his waist, the others all carried only spears of some kind so Fellyn assumed this closest man must be in charge. She hadn't seen much of their faces and they seemed so alike. Feigning sleep, she kept her eyes half closed while watching the men, the fear accompanying her desire to flee was overwhelming. Her little sister was still leaning uncomfortably against her shoulder and though exhausted, she dare not sleep for fear of attack from the men. She was tied to her sister at the feet and running seemed impossible. The cave was dark and what little light the fire threw out wasn't reaching their little dark corner of rock, Fellyn looked around her feet, searching for a sharp rock, moving her feet gently she pulled rocks towards her and her eye caught a pointed rock which seemed sharp enough to try. She nudged her sister gently and her head rose with a small start "shhh" Fellyn whispered and slowly moved to reach for the rock, straightened up looking at the men, they hadn't seen. She gently slid her hands to her feet, her back aching terribly and her whole body cold through her cloak. She started using the flint to saw at the bindings on their feet, starting with her sister's, once it broke through she glanced at the men again but they were ignoring the helpless little girls. Fellyn smiled encouragingly at her sister and as their eyes met, her sister's name suddenly flashed across her mind, Althia.

A merge of moments ran through her, broken ropes, a sword, her sister's beautiful smile and a hand under a sheet of thick ice.

Leaning on the door for support, her mind cleared and she realised the water had reached her breast. Struggling to calm her panic, Fellyn swam to the door she had not tried and seeing it pulled inwards like the others, she decided to try and stem the flow rather than exit. A mad plan perhaps, but she swam slowly, breaking the ice with her hands as she went, it was still thin like a small film but as she worked her way toward the grating, which was completely under the water, the ice grew thicker and she realised she had nothing with which to block the flow of ice water. Her body temperature dropping lower, her mind was fogging when she remembered the wooden chair which had Nephi carved into it, she turned back to the chair and saw it was already bobbing along the water, she pulled it and found she had little strength for that, so swam behind the chair and pushed it along the water. She was nearing the grate when she realised that there was nothing with which to tie the chair to the grate's covering. But it didn't make sense, why would the grate cracking stop the water from draining to the other side of the river bed? Realisation flooded her foggy mind and she saw that in fact the other grate had been blocked, her mind so preoccupied with the broken grating she hadn't thought to fix the other instead.

Swimming fiercely through to the other side, and leaving the carved chair to its fate, she drew in breath and sucked up her fear of the ice and allowed herself to submerge. Through the crystal clear room, but with light from the ceiling window fading, she swam in closer to the grate and seeing that in fact, it was a body blocking the grate, she panicked. Dread. Deep fear and uncertainty filled her but she pushed her body hard and got to the limp figure that she found, pulled the arm free that had been sucked into the grating and yanked the limp body out of the pull of the water. As soon as she felt the body move under her, she noticed the drag from the grating intensify, emptying the room of its contents but dragging her in. With the weight of the lifeless, male body in her arms, she was drowning under the ice. Somehow, instinct pushed her and she kicked her legs harder and harder, pushing her body to beyond its limit to free herself and this man she held in one arm. Fellyn's head broke the surface of the thin ice and the air flooded into her lungs in one desperate gulp of oxygen, she pulled the man's head up too but holding them both afloat was all she could manage so she simply waited until the water was dropping to move. The carved chair, pulled with the current, floated towards them and she grabbed hold for aid, her feet now touching the floor but the water still up to her chest. She shoved the man unceremoniously onto the chair and silently wondered if he was alive. Slowly the water level lowered, giving her the ability to kneel and she set herself to trying to figure out the fate of the man before her, leaning against the carved chair. She put her head to his chest and heard nothing. Fellyn raised her fist high and pounded it down on his chest several times and opening his mouth she blew air into his lungs. She had no idea whether it would work but was imitating an action she had seen someone carry out on one of the children who had fallen into the stream which flowed through Tebel. His eyes flew open and water sprayed from his mouth like a fountain, he choked and spluttered and Fellyn simply leaned away.

Fellyn was utterly shocked by the presence of a man who somehow she had just saved from a terrible fate, not to mention her own too. After vomiting water repeatedly, the man leaned down onto the chair, the floor was still soaked but it was a puddle rather than a swamp so she lay her hand down on his forehead and moved the thick blond hair from his eyes. He tilted his head to look up at her and weakly smiled "Who is this angel sent to save me?" he croaked.

"I'm…lost actually. I wasn't aware you were here until it happened" she said, cold and confusion surrounding her already broken concentration.

"Neither was I" he said "and…what did happen?"

Fellyn just stared around the strange room, *water arena*, she thought and pondered whether this was designed to happen for entertainment. "I'm not sure, I was searching the castle and came in here, then the room flooded, I had no idea you were there but you were stuck in the grate and when I pulled you free the room emptied again…" Fellyn babbled quickly, running through the events in her mind, trying desperately to make sense of it all. The fear and the memories of her sister, Althia returned and she gasped, vaguely piecing together what had happened and fearing that her sister had been taken by ice.

"Well I'm thankful for God sending an angel my way!" the man laughed, coughing again and looking about him. "How do we get out?" he asked.

"Well I know how I got in…but the other doors wouldn't open." Fellyn said cautiously, she really had no idea who this person was, he hadn't offered a name and she felt wary of offering hers. The moment of elation of his survival had passed, and she was frightened of his strong arms and penetrating blue eyes. All adrenaline calming in her exhausted body, she began to shiver from being cold and terrified.

He looked around and said "I haven't a clue how I got here, so choose a path and I'll follow dear maiden" and rising to his feet, dripping wet, she saw that he was tall. Tall and broad like a powerful tree, he looked to be older than Fellyn, but couldn't be more than a few years her senior.

She stood, pushing her dark hair behind her ears and wringing out the ends, she looked down at the bluebell robe and wished she were back in the warmth of the garden. Walking towards the door she had entered through, she felt his strong presence close behind her, she pulled open the left hand door easily but when they passed through it, the corridor was very different to the one she had come through originally. Disoriented and dazed, she looked around the high ceiling and long corridor, it was only partially covered, with glass-less windows all along the length of the walkway, leading to grass outside, it was not the courtyard at all, there were no flowers and not a glimpse of sun under the blanket of cloud and fog. "Oh." She sighed. "This is not the way I came…"

"Well we're out, and nowhere near water so lets keep on the path." He said confidently, he didn't seem afraid of this peculiar place at all. "What a bulwark though, it is the most labyrinthine place I have ever explored!" Fellyn looked at him, astonished, what did that mean?

"You, you're a traveller?" she asked timidly.

"Well, yes, actually. I have been all over Xandia in search of my lost love! I have travelled mountains and glades, desert and town in my search, never have I seen a place such as this, truly remarkable!" He exclaimed excitedly. "And certainly, dear maiden, I have never been rescued by such a lovely lady, tell me, what is your name?"

"Fellyn. And yours?" She said, blushing at his comments.

"I am Blake" he said confidently. "So, my beautiful companion, Fellyn, shall we carry on the path in search of an exit together? I'd hate to leave such a vulnerable maiden all alone." He winked at her, and offered her his arm.

"Thank you, sir, I would rather walk unaided…but I would be glad of the company."

He shrugged and stood by her side and together they followed the long corridor through the fog.

A door stood at the end of the corridor, inlaid with symbols similar to those in the under passage, Fellyn touched their carved swirls and images, wondering what it could all mean.

"Flag Arena." Blake stated, looking at the words written on a plaque on the door.

"Another arena...oh I wouldn't go in...." Fellyn started, appalled that there was another arena besides the watery hell she had just faced. But Blake did not listen. He had turned the ring handle and pushed before Fellyn had finished speaking and the two were faced with a room which was extremely long and fairly thin. Blake stepped in, and

Fellyn looked behind her, realising that she could see nothing through the foggy windows and was not prepared to enter the water arena again, so she simply followed the stranger against her better judgement.

After she had crossed the doorway, the slam behind her told both of them that they would be unable to return the way they had come. It really was a stunning room, with high walls adorned with hundreds of hung family crests and shields, flags, banners and bunting. Golden torch bearers stood every few feet, dressed in heavy golden armour and completely immobile but their torches burned and flickered in the dark room. The whole place had a passage feel to it for aside from the torch bearing suits of armour, there was no other furniture nor standing objects on the floor, and the large stones which had been lain in no pattern across the floor were indented with carved family crests similar to some on the high walls. Fellyn let out the breath she had been holding, frightened for this arena's mysteries and for the unknown quantity that was the man beside her. Strangely, she found herself wishing it were Jared with her instead for the safety of something familiar, whether forboding or not.

"Stay here, maiden, I wish to figure out the place!" Blake winked, clearly enjoying his time here. He stepped out onto one of the crested stones, depicting a badger, crossed swords and two types of plant in the four quadrants. Nothing happened. Blake turned again and winked at Fellyn, then moved on to a stone which had no carving on its face. As his rear foot left the crested stone for the plain one, each of the suits of armour took a large step, each in a different direction but each swinging a great sword to both sides as they went. Some of the swords clanked against walls but most just sang as they whipped through the air. Blake was a good few feet away from any of the suits of armour, but he stood completely still on the plain stone, both feet firmly planted and not daring to move again.

Fellyn just stood, mouth slightly parted and eyes wide at the scene before her, puzzling in her mind the relevance of the crests on the stones and the placement of the suits of armour.

"Oh good, a game!" Blake said to the aghast woman over his shoulder. He held out his hand to her, and she backed away, her body pressed into the door behind her. "Come on, there is no exit behind you and the only other door is this way, live dangerously or die maiden!" He said jokingly and grinned at her, showing his perfect smile and roguish eyes. She stepped forwards, not wanting to touch any stone save the ones he had so she stepped with one foot on to the badger and crossed sword crest stone, keeping the other foot on her original standing point, every suit of armour took a large steps again, slashing the air as they went and turning to different directions. She pulled her other foot to the stone with a squeak and once firmly placed, the torchbearers stopped. Blake tilted his head, looked up at the high walls, feet still planted firmly on the spot he stood on, and leaned forward slightly to see where the nearest torchbearer had stood before moving.

"I...I think they move to the same crest you do..." He said, eyebrows pulled tightly together in his thoughts.

"Stay where you are a moment, maiden." Blake turned and stepped on a stone which depicted four Fleur De Lis and a clover, when one foot was firmly planted on the stone the torchbearers began moving again stepping on to stones and swiping their swords back and forth, one coming dangerously close to Blake as he ducked and drew his second foot on to the stone. Blake was two small stones away from the torchbearer now, he looked at where it had stepped and up at the wall again, then back to the torchbearer before him, it had words written on its back "Cheile." He read out. The stones had not matched his choice, in fact they had followed no pattern at all, treading on random stones it seemed.

Fellyn, too, was puzzling their situation out, but remembering the dragons on the carvings, wondered if the castle crest was somewhere in here and studied the crests around her for dragons. There was one a few stones to her left so she jumped on to it, both feet planted firmly at once and she smiled as she realised nothing had happened.

"Blake!" She cried. "Try to find the dragon crest." She said, realising that she had jumped without checking he was ready for the torchbearer to move. He looked around him and saw one just behind the golden suit. He leaped on to it in one fluid motion and the torchbearer was still. Blake grinned.

"You might be on it, maiden, try another!" Blake said to her encouragingly. There was another dragon crest diagonally up from the place she stood so she stepped her foot on to it more delicately, Blake ducked as with a clank, the torchbearer spun the sword around and turned to walk to the right. Blake wobbled on the step, on all fours so as not to get in the way of the sword. Fellyn had stood still on the crested stone but was confused about the torchbearers, she had been sure of the dragons being the right choice.

She was still not far from Blake and she did not want to be left behind, trying to puzzle out the room alone, so she shouted "I'm coming to join you, stay down!" and when Blake nodded confirmation, she jumped the few stones distance until she stood two away from Blake who had needed to step back twice to move away from the suit.

Blake stood again once the torchbearer had stopped and the pair looked at each other as they each tried to figure out how to move further. They were moving slowly up the very long room and there were more than fifteen suits dotted along the room that they could see, they needed to understand what made the torchbearers move. Something clicked in Blake's mind, he decided to test a theory so he leaped with both feet to the stone beside him so that he was on the crest beside Fellyn. As both feet landed, he looked around. The suits were still immobile so he smiled at Fellyn and said "there must be two feet on the stone, maiden, not one. You need to jump not step." Blake demonstrated by jumping with both feet to the stone in front of him and the silence of the immobile torchbearers proved his point. Fellyn leaped with both feet so that she was still beside him, frightened to be left alone.

"But what about the crests?" She asked, bewildered.

"I...I'm not sure if it tells us where they move, there are too many!" Blake said, and he jumped forward again so that he was fairly close to another torchbearer, it was facing him straight on this time and it unnerved him how it seemed to be looking at him through the thick golden helmet. Fellyn exhaled, realising she had been holding her breath for quite a while and she used both feet to jump forwards, watching Blake and the torchbearer rather than her footing. As she landed, her right foot touched the stone just beside the one she had aimed for and in that moment, the torchbearers stepped into life, thrusting their swords wildly from side to side. Blake moved away just in time, throwing himself backwards which caused the torchbearers to step in random directions until he could scramble up to standing firmly on one stone. Fellyn was crouched down, only a stone away from another torchbearer and too terrified to move again. They had reached almost half way through the room and Blake could see their exit now, blocked somewhat by the torchbearers dotted around, and he could see that there was an hourglass dangling about a foot away from the door, sand streaming into the lower chamber and almost running out from the top. Blake did not want to find out what happened when the timer ran out, he grabbed Fellyn's hand and leaning forwards, pulled her to standing.

"Trust me now maiden, and we will get out just fine. Jump to the stone I stand on." He said plainly, lowering his head so that making eye contact was inevitable.

Fellyn simply nodded, unsure what he would ask of her and she sprang over to the stone, pressing her body far too close to his in order to stand together on the small area. "When I move my foot, you keep the other of yours planted firm and move the same as I do, mirror me. We need to move exactly at the same time and we can make it across the room, got it?" Blake asked, speaking slowly for her to understand in her worried state.

"Yes." Fellyn choked out, terrified of the torchbearers all around them which seemed to be buzzing with a held breath, waiting for the pair to fail. Blake used his right hand to tap her left leg, "ready?" He asked. Fellyn nodded again and looking down at her feet, stepped in time with Blake to the stone beside theirs, then as he spoke the word again, they pulled their other feet to standing on the new stone. It worked brilliantly, they would just need to be cautious of stones which were too small for them both to stand on, which was a fair amount, Blake noted as he glanced around their path. They stepped like this a few paces and had to stop and duck down when Blake's heel caught a rough stone as they were pulling their feet together.

When they stood again, Fellyn smiled as if the whole thing were a game and said "it's just like dancing, really!" She laughed a little, causing Blake to grin at her in return. They continued their dance, matching each other's pace and ducking when needed when suddenly Blake noticed how low the sand was. He gasped and tried to show Fellyn, they hurried a little and caused a reaction of scything and whistling from the torchbearers around them and their wasted time spent dodging these meant that they didn't notice the sand stop running. Fellyn felt as if her world were closing in, she assumed she was dizzy from being too close to Blake and ducking down so fast, and then realised that it wasn't her mind causing the room to appear to close in on them. The whole room was shrinking thinner and thinner, threatening to crush them if they did not manage the last distance. Blake pulled Fellyn and brought her feet on to his own, he stepped sideways awkwardly like a crab, holding her waist tightly in his arm and stepped long strides across the room, not bothering to duck from scything swords but just darting around them and dropping Fellyn, held her hand and yelled "RUN!" instead. They reached the door and threw their weight against it, falling ungracefully to the room beyond.

Chapter 6 – Killing Time

Nephi watched Fellyn and Blake as they recovered and moved away from the trial they had just faced, he saw the lack of conversation and simply smiled. Deciding to help her remember further, he disappeared back into the thick fog and sent another trial her way.

Blake watched Fellyn as she walked beside him, she had barely uttered a word since they had escaped the room with the crests, they had moved through the castle quickly and quietly, trying to find an exit and thankfully finding no more arena rooms. She was determined and shy, forcing them both to move deeper in her desperation to find some courtyard she had mentioned, saying if she found that courtyard, she would find a way out. The thick fog blocked their ability to get their bearings by looking outside, Blake frowned out of the nearest window, trying to see anything besides the wall of grey mist that surrounded the castle. Nothing. He sighed and set back to talking, since Fellyn wasn't forthcoming with conversation, he was talking enough for the both of them.

"So where are you from, Fellyn? I come from a village north of the mountain range, so very different from here. I find it so empty in these forests and I miss the sunshine as the thick trees don't allow much through, do they?" No response. He kept trying, persistent and keen to know more about this woman.

"I'd bet my hat you're from one of the villages around here, I wouldn't guess you for a travelling girl and you're a bit…uptight here…no offence." He looked at her, she had stopped walking and was looking at him with something like irritation.

"You, sir, are not wearing a hat." She stated bluntly, lifted one eyebrow, then turned and continued walking.

Blake blinked, caught up and laughingly pulled out his still damp pockets, his knife was inside one, unharmed, but the scabbard was full of water, he emptied it out and tried the other pocket only to find it empty. He had lost the token he kept of his love.

Blake stopped in his tracks and looked about him, realising that the only precious thing he kept with him had gone and most likely into the water, with no way of retrieving it. He sighed, accepted its loss and allowed his mind to wander to the girl he hunted for.

"Left or right here?" Fellyn asked him, with a grimace. "I think we may have been here before…" She sighed.

"It all looks the same to me. Right then? We have been going left more than right." Blake commented, he saw Fellyn consider this, she had not noticed her preference for turning left until now, but it was obviously a flaw as they could be travelling in a circle.

"Right it is then!" Fellyn said, she smiled at Blake, not wanting to show him her weakness.

They walked along the corridor, seeing the same bricks and windows at every turn, she was getting frustrated when they passed through an archway into a small sub-room with large, high double doors on the opposite wall.

"At last!" Blake exclaimed brightly, he moved towards them incautiously and lifted the large latches, shoving the door as he did so, the doors creaked loudly and swung forwards allowing them access to a chamber with a stunning painted dome ceiling. A very large table ran the length of the room with two large carved chairs seated at either end.

"Wow!" Blake breathed, she was beside him now, in awe of the room before her.

"It's stunning." Fellyn said, and having looked long enough for her own liking, she moved through the room to the door to the right of the table. Blake slowly followed, turning in circles to admire the ceiling above them. She smiled at his admiration for the room, thinking it pleasant to meet someone appreciative of beauty.

Walking through the door they found yet another corridor, but this time overlooking the courtyard that Fellyn had remembered. As it was foggy, the warmth and beauty was not so permeating, but it was still a lovely sight to behold and she gasped as the realisation that she was no longer lost filled her with hope.

"Oh!" Fellyn exclaimed, she turned to Blake's stunned face and said excitedly, "this is it, this is the courtyard I remembered!"

Blake just smiled back at her and gestured for her to lead the way, they followed the walkway around to the break in the wall and entered the courtyard with its stunning blooms and pond, Fellyn went to the pond and saw her own clothes hanging on the wall where she had left them. She cupped her hand into the water and drank, dipping her hands again and again to satiate her thirst. Blake had other ideas, right in front of Fellyn, he stripped down to nothing and slipped himself into the cool water. Fellyn turned her head as soon as she realised what he was doing and raised her hand to block her vision with a little squeak, she had only caught a glimpse of his torso which was muscular and sculpted. A fierce heat of embarrassment worked its way up her face and chest. Picking up her clothes, she wandered away to admire the bluebells once more, Blake laughed and dipped his head under the water, drinking deeply of the pool and raising his head up again, smiling at Fellyn's modest response to his actions. He allowed himself to bob in the water and enjoyed its almost warm feel against his skin, it tasted spectacular, like the purest of all things.

Fellyn was bending to admire a patch of daffodils when she heard Blake rising, she turned around more so as not to see his nakedness, and waited until he had come to stand beside her again before she spoke. "Isn't it beautiful…the garden I mean…" She blushed deeply.

"Simply divine!" Blake laughed back. "I am dressed dear maiden, you can look again" he chuckled. Fellyn smiled at him shyly.

"I think we should go this way, I remember it leading towards the tower I stayed in last night." Fellyn said with determination, she just desired nothing more than to leave this place and find Etana but she needed to find Nephi, and that was the last place she had seen him so returning seemed sensible, since he wasn't in the garden. Blake smiled and followed as Fellyn walked towards the stairs on the opposite corridor, going up the stairs led to yet another plain corridor and she followed it to the right this time, trying each door she found at the top of a flight of stairs. Eventually she found the one which was familiar and rose up the stairs, Blake on her heels.

When she opened the door she realised the bed of furs had been re-made. It was immaculate, as if she had not spent the night here at all, but it was exactly the same, with the chair Nephi had sat in still perched by the door. Fellyn sighed. Walking to the window she could see the patch of grime which was smudged from where she had wiped it with her hand and felt her disappointment at not finding Nephi.

"So…don't you know how to get out of here, you must remember how you got in…" Fellyn said, turning to Blake. She had taken the lead on their journey through the castle and he had simply allowed her to lead with no questions or comments.

"No, I remember entering a gatehouse to speak with a curiously blue man and then remember waking up in the water with you." He smiled at her, as if the memory of their near death was something to smile about. He didn't seem at all perturbed by the memory of this and it rattled at Fellyn, who had been affected by that water arena more than she would care to admit.

"Nothing at all?" she asked, desperate.

"No, sweet maiden. I remember only the gatehouse, a man, well...possibly a man...asking my name and my business here and after telling him these I remember nothing but waking to your pretty face." Blake grinned at her, teasing her with flattery and irritating her with a lack of information. Disgruntled, she turned back to the door, walked around Blake and found the door shut. And locked. Pulling harder on the handle, she wriggled it around and shoved with all her strength. Blake looked at her actions, only mildly concerned, and figuring her to be moving it the wrong way he gently touched her shoulder, moved her aside and then tried the door himself. It moved not an inch and he gave up, flung himself into the chair and sighed. Fellyn looked at him, irritated that he had given up so easily and she marched over to stand in front of the strange man.

"Why are you not breaking down the door?" She questioned.

"Maiden it is locked, somebody has locked us in, and like our experience in the water and crest room, we most likely will have to perform in some way in order to be freed so if I were you, I should sit and calm yourself." Blake said.

"But...who?!" Fellyn asked, astonished at his relaxed composure at the present situation.

"Most likely the odd blue fellow who seems to have erased my memory and tried to drown us both." He sighed, "now, maiden, even if you are not tired I think I should like to sleep. I will leave you the bed as the gentleman that I am." He said, and getting himself slouched into the wooden chair, he shut his eyes. Fellyn moved to the bed and sat down on it, frustrated and embarrassed. She felt a chill and needed comfort so wrapped a fur around her shoulders, watched Blake and asked "you mentioned a lost love, Blake, who is she?"

Blake raised his head with his boyish smile playing on his lips, "a girl I have loved all of my life. We were children playing together, and our mothers had already pre-arranged our betrothal before she was even five years old. We were schooled together by tutors, and played music together, she was my very dearest friend and the most beautiful of girls anyone had ever seen." He was smiling at his memory, lost in his thoughts of the girl who lived in his heart.

"Where is she?" Fellyn questioned softly.

Blake smiled with a flicker of pain on his face, "well, dear maiden, if I knew where she was, I would not have been searching the lands for her."

Fellyn fell silent, to be so loved as to have someone devote their whole life to finding you, what would that feel like?

"Anyway Fellyn, I should rather like to know more of you, I feel I have spoken most between us and know nothing of who you are." He grinned again and leaned forward for her answer.

"I was raised by a woman not my mother, in the village of Tebel not many miles from here. I married young, to the best hunter of our village and we have been together only a year or so, since we wed, that is." Fellyn said with a bored sigh, she decided not to divulge about her lost daughter in case he was a threat.

"Then why are you all alone my sweet girl, in such a place?" Blake questioned.

"Well, if you must know, I was walking the area and fell into a hole by the castle entrance and Nephi brought me to the garden and then to this room. I am as confused by my being here as you are." Fellyn said.

"Oh, I see, where is your husband then my dear, for he must be worried for you." Blake said, concerned.

Fellyn smirked inwardly, *no, he is hunting me and has tried to kill me*, she thought to herself.

"My husband does not know where I am. He is hunting." Fellyn answered, cutting the truth and changing it into a vague answer.

Blake scrutinised her for a moment, deep in concentration. Slowly he got up and moved from the chair to the foot of the bed, Fellyn drew herself further away and then relaxed, Blake was sitting on the edge of the bed, facing the window. "If I were your husband, my lady, I would hunt night and day to find you and bring you safely home." He was trying to be comforting, but he was simply rubbing salt in the wounds she felt opening raw inside her, she had been ignoring her emotions about Jared and had set her heart of stone on simply finding a way out of her predicament and getting back to where she once lived.

"Well I guess that is the sort of man you are, not all are like you though, Blake" Fellyn responded, hurt.

"No, not all are" he said, and sensing pain in her eyes, he turned his head towards her. "Who are you running from, Fellyn, yourself or your husband?" He breathed quietly.

Caught, Fellyn dropped her eyes, feeling tears sting at her and not knowing what to say, she had always hidden Jared's faults from everyone, even Tehya, and she had no friends in the village, not really.

Here sat a man with a sense for pain and he had seen right through her, what else could he see of her?

"He...he gets angry with me...but I know he loves me..." Fellyn said, feeling herself yet again defending a man who had tried to kill her and their child. It burned her heart again as she angrily wondered why exactly she did protect his honour.

"No woman deserves to be living in fear; it's you he hunts then, my lady?" Blake said bluntly. He turned to face Fellyn and moved closer to her.

"Yes. I have taken his daughter, our daughter." Fellyn babbled, suddenly tears fell from her eyes, rushing down into her lap and she tasted the salty stream on her lips. "When I fell into the hole I had left her in the grass, she is all alone and for all I know has been taken by someone, him even. And I cannot stay here, Blake, I am terrified that she will be taken it is killing me to think of her in danger while I rest here!" Fellyn was shouting herself hoarse, her body trembling as she sobbed and her heart overwhelmed with dread.

Blake simply reached for her hand and took it in both of his, he stroked her hair and under his breath said "as you have saved me, sweet maiden, so I shall protect you and your little one."

Fellyn looked at him, questioning her sanity for allowing herself to break down on a stranger, but she felt safe with Blake after everything the had been through in that one day, and he was a man of his word. If he would search all the land for years to find a lost love, perhaps he truly would protect her.

"Fellyn, my dear, did Nephi not tell you of the magic this place holds?" Blake breathed into her ear.

Fellyn snorted, laughing at the notion.

"No, really, time stands still in this place, so while here your daughter is safe, until you leave its grounds you shall not see time pass." He smiled at her, expecting her to be relieved but seeing only concern. Fellyn had questions, plenty of them, but she allowed herself to be comforted by this strange man and his strange tales.

"Tell me about the mountains, Blake?" Fellyn asked.

Blake smiled, released her hand and as she sank back on to the furs, he spoke softly of the mountain folk and their different ways, of the thinner air and the smell of coming snow. He spoke of Lords and Ladies of the realm and of a beauty in the people. Fellyn drifted to sleep listening to his gentle, deep voice and when she was deep in slumber, Blake tucked the furs around her, removed a red velvet blanket for himself and returned to his chair to rest.

Chapter 7 – Loneliness

Tehya shifted her position ever so slightly, she was peering through trees to where Jared sat on a small pile of rocks by the river. He was eating an apple which was over-ripe and slightly fermented, Tehya could smell the sour fruit from her hiding place. She had been tracking Jared for a day and a half and he seemed to be on a trail of sorts, most likely it was Fellyn's, but they couldn't be certain since rain had fallen it was harder to see tracks or signs of movement. Jared had caught a slight muddy paw print in some soft earth nearer the water's edge and had followed the direction so Tehya felt fairly certain of his tracking skills. She was surprising herself, being old and there was no point denying it, she knew her tracking days were limited, when a person was creaking as they walked and shuffling to keep the limp less painful it was harder to be stealthy. Luckily, while Jared was a great tracker, he had no fear about him and was not on guard for disturbance and so had not noticed the clear signs that he was being followed.

Tehya was keeping a fair distance, tracking him closely and when he stopped to rest, she would double back and rest herself, she had built no fires but was wrapped thickly with cloaks and was adept at finding food in the forest for she had lived there all of her long life. She was busying herself filling pockets with nuts from the bush through which she peered when she saw a large patch of disturbed earth under the branches by her feet. A thick clump of grey-brown fur was matted onto a patch of thorns beside it and Tehya smiled, Fellyn was a survivor and it would take Jared quite a lot of wiles to keep up with such a girl.

Jared was stoking the little fire he had made, but the drizzling rain was proving to be a nuisance as it was turning his fire into a smoky half-flame. He was trying to cook a small bird on a long stick but the pathetic fire was making this difficult. He stoked his fire and deciding to give up, he curled himself close to the fire in his thin cloak and fell asleep. Tehya moved backwards out of the bushes and moved quietly back to a thick clump of trees she had spotted a way back. Once there she busied herself with a rock and the nuts, drinking from her wineskin and shaking it to check the water contents but realising she was low, returned it to her pocket and carried on eating.

After a few handfuls of the nuts to calm her growling belly she settled herself on a thick pile of autumn leaves and pulled her cloaks around her head and body, like a thick cocoon. Said a quick prayer of blessing and protection for Fellyn, Etana and Jared and then fell asleep.

Upon awakening, she could hear Jared's voice. She moved into the deepest bush she could find and waited, thankfully she had heard him talking angrily to himself or she would not have moved in time, he trod right where she had been lying not moments before and again thanked God for her sense to hide the nut shells. He moved through the tree clump and turned once on the other side, so that he was walking along a thick fallen tree serving as a small bridge across the river and onto the other side, once he was a fair distance ahead, Tehya moved out, filled her wineskin at the river bed and creakily got up to follow him over the makeshift-bridge and on to the other bank. Her bones ached as usual, and she could feel her knees weakening with all the walking. As she trudged the forest following Jared's easy trail, she thought of home and of her guests, Rhia had agreed to watch the goat for a few days and was glad of the milk Tehya had said she was welcome to take from Grissy and have for her family, the cats would fend for themselves. The hens would be in more danger of predators but they would scavenge bugs just fine without her, as long as they didn't take to eating their own eggs again the daft girls!

Tehya was noting Jared's direction, he was headed east towards the biggest town in the area, but Tehya knew Fellyn well, if she were running from her life in Tebel, and Tehya knew full well what would have her running, then she would be searching for her past and that would lead her to the mountains. Jared was going in the wrong direction. The mountains were northwest of their village, Tehya knew that the only way both Fellyn and Jared could be happy was together and she was determined to help this man fix his marriage and bring home his precious wife. So when Jared settled to sleep that evening, Tehya was going to plant tracks for him to follow, leading him northwest instead. She smiled to herself and began planning what to leave for him.

Jared was a way ahead, muttering to himself again, this angry man was consumed with self-doubt and he desperately missed his wife, that much was clear, but Tehya did not understand fully why he was such an angry person. Jared's own father was a beloved man of the village, and his mother was still the local mother hen, people took to her hands when readying for a birth, since she had had so many live births of her own they trusted her judgement, she was a kind and gentle woman with a heart of gold. She had raised her children very well, so well that Jared, the oldest had too become a man loved in the village. He was kind and considerate of the villagers, going out of his way to serve their needs, bringing water to those less mobile, hunting large amounts of quarry so he could feed the vulnerable and so on. He was part of the village council and was very respected. But Tehya saw through his kindness to the others, she saw his love for Fellyn, but also how he spent his time, he did not cherish his wife, and he preferred company of others to Fellyn's. Tehya felt wounded that since their marriage a year or so back, Fellyn had withdrawn into a shy and fearful girl again after blossoming into such a friendly and sweet woman. Since having Etana, Fellyn had been more broken than the day she had

72

arrived in Tebel with know real knowledge of herself. Tehya sighed and watched the man who had broken her loving child, God would call him up on his mistakes, but Tehya had often wished she were able to do that herself for it would give her such a pleasure to see that man brought to sense and see his errors.

Dusk was drawing close, Tehya had barely eaten today, so when Jared lit his little fire again, she decided to test her stealth once more. Jared had sat by the fire for a long time, quiet and motionless staring into the flames, and after a long time, he had fallen asleep further from the fire than before. Tehya walked quietly into his camping area and slipped a perch wrapped in thick leaves onto the smouldering branches. She moved onwards, the way she assumed Jared would travel next and after a few hundred yards she found a muddy patch, she bent down, groaning as she did so for the pain in her hips and knees, and traced a paw print shape into the mud. It looked distorted but it would do. She then unlaced her boot and placed her naked foot into the mud, giggling like a little girl, she did the same with the other, then wiped both clean on the grassy patches to her right and slipped back into her stockings and boots again. She crept back to Jared's camp, she had been gone an hour or so and he slept as soundly as he had been before, she smirked at her ingenuity and pulled the hot leaf-covered fish from the fire. Carrying it in cool leaves she had taken from an oak nearby, and took it back again to her own resting place under a large willow by the river. She ate the perch happily, its smoky flesh was delicious after days of roughage in the forest. If Jared was so oblivious to her presence she could possibly afford more confidence to observe him! Smiling at her luck again, and at the beauty of the night sky, she buried the fish bones, head and tail under the patch of decaying leaves to her side. She hummed the River song to herself, a tale of a woman borne of water and entrancing to men who called to them from their slumber and opened their minds to read like a page of written word. Tehya smiled at the beauty of the place she rested, marvelling at its resemblance to the song and thanked God for the season of this occurrence between the Kellacks. She praying again for safety of all involved and in her peace, Tehya slipped into a dreamless sleep.

As day broke, Tehya woke and moved to the river, she splashed cool water on her face and arms and unlaced her boots again, she washed them in the river, removing the mud from last night's events and amused at herself again, she re-dressed and moved out towards Jared's camp again, munching on a late plum as she went, picking out the stone and a small worm along the way.

Jared had already moved on, but his fire was recently doused and a few twigs snapped in the direction she had assumed he would go. She followed again, thankful for her prediction of his movements and when, some time later, she came to the spot where her own bare feet left tracks, she smiled seeing his boot print beside the hand made paw print. He had changed direction following the one pointed by her own foot. Chuckling to herself and checking the area for signs of his hanging back, she followed on, needing to see how far ahead she was moving so as to gauge where to place herself. The mountains would be a good six days walk at least from the village, and with their slight detour, if she could keep him on track, he may even stand a chance at catching up to Fellyn. Tehya contemplated going home, and trusting that God would save their marriage when they were reunited, but she did not want to risk danger for Fellyn if Jared's temper was raised at her when he found her, so Tehya followed on again and kept her distance safer. Watching him from further away and trying not to keep him from thinking of anything but his own actions.

Rhia was sat at their table, the fire casting a warm glow on the walls and stealing her gaze so she was mesmerised by its magic. The door bumped into the log basket sat by the door and made Rhia jump,

Cassius stepped into the room from the cooler night outside and stamped his boots, removing his travelling cloak and hat and then unlacing his boots to come and relax.

"Welcome home, dear, I thought you would be much later getting back!" Rhia said, standing and moving to where his dinner of salted fish and bread sat waiting for him. Rhia was nervous, Cassius had not heard about Jared disappearing since he had gone to Cabaro for two days, leaving on the last night she had seen Jared. Cassius would most likely be irritated that he had asked the local men to help build the Kellacks a new house when Jared was nowhere to be found nor helping the effort.

"Weather was good, a little damp but well enough for me to travel faster than normal." He sniffed at the food and smiled at Rhia. "Would you be a dear and rub Storm down, I pushed her hard to get back, then I have news for you!" Cassius was in a very good mood, so Rhia nodded and headed out into the dark evening. Storm was their mare, a sturdy girl who was getting on in years but did the light journey to Cabaro nicely for Cassius, Rhia had been thinking it would soon be time to find another but she wanted to keep Storm to teach the boys to ride well, her steadiness was a great asset in teaching the boys but Cassius often had her travelling with him so Rhia didn't have a lot of time to spare with Storm. Perhaps she would suggest he look for a younger travelling horse when he was next in the town, since he was in high spirits today he would probably be happy with the idea. Rhia rubbed the old girl down and brushed her fine mane with the heavy bristled brush, Storm snorted gently and tossed her head a little, she had never liked being brushed much. Laying down the brush, Rhia untied Storm's rope from the post it was on and led the fine horse around to the pen at the back of the house, she remembered that Grissy was out there and hoped the two would get on well. She untied the rope from Storm and released her from the bit in her teeth, Storm chomped happily on the air and wandered over to the hay bale under the shelter, there was a small scuffle of feet as the two animals adjusted to each other and found a place, then they went quiet to eat and rest.

Rhia left them to settle and started back for the house, grabbing a loaded log basket on the way in.

Cassius had already cleared eaten his fill and was putting his plate in the washing bowl when Rhia came in, she kicked the empty log basket out of it's place by the door and clumsily dropped the full one down.

Cassius sat heavily on the chair he liked to occupy, nearest the fire and hand carved with fine detail.

"So, the news from Cabaro is that they want me to go to Varose soon. Tobias has been keeping me informed so I hadn't needed to go more than every summer and I'm certain the old dog was stopping me going on purpose, he's a sly one...been trying to weasel his way closer to Darue for a long time but they see through him...anyway dear they asked for me to go there for a meeting in a few days time." Rhia had been listening while stacking a few logs in the fire, she sat back on her heels from where she knelt and looked up at her husband. There was always a part of Rhia that enjoyed her time with the boys when Cassius was away, but having him leave for Varose more often would be different, it was a good couple of weeks travel each time, and if he needed to stay for extra meetings it would be longer. But then again, getting closer to Darue was no bad thing, he was a generous leader and lavished gifts on those close to him who he could trust, so Cassius being favoured would bring them all blessing surely.

"Do you know why they have asked for you so soon, is it urgent?" Rhia asked, thinking of the house that would probably not be finished while Cassius was away. "And how long will you be gone?" She smiled, trying to show her support and concern in equal measure.

"Oh I don't know dear, weeks most likely, they didn't say a reason. I assume it is important but Tobias didn't know why so I won't know until I get there!" Cassius leaned down to his wife on their cobbled floor and patted her hair, "You could ask Fellyn and Jared if they'd like to stay here with you while I'm gone if you're worried for company, I'd bet that they're cramped over at his mother's place."

Rhia looked at her lap, dreading telling him that they were all missing.

"Actually, Jared hasn't been seen since a few days back when he saw the house...Fellyn still hasn't come back either...if she even got out of the house..." Rhia finished quietly. Cassius sat back and sighed.

"I don't think she was in the house when it burned, I believe Obe saw her running away she will be fine sweetheart...don't you worry. As for Jared...if he has gone to find her then I say he's being a good man, better get her home safe than sit here waiting!" Cassius smiled, comforting Rhia a little, it would be very lonely when her husband was gone.

Chapter 8 – Reservations and Fear

Blake was pacing the little room, very aware of his feet and how unattached they seemed to him. Odd things, feet. He was trying not to make too much noise as he walked, Fellyn was still sleeping and he guessed it to have been about six hours since they fell asleep. He had been watching her sleep for the past twenty minutes or so, she was angelic resting there surrounded by the furs and velvet. He smiled at her and felt a surge of protective emotion at this broken woman before him. Thoughts filled his mind of how best to punish the husband if he ever showed his face. Blake laughed at himself, attached to a woman he had just met and he hadn't even been to bed with her, not in the way that was usual to him. He thought of the possibility of spending a careless night with Fellyn, as if she were any other girl he met on his journey, and he couldn't picture it, as if it weren't even vaguely a possibility. It wasn't as if he had never been with a married woman before, there had been the vicar's wife in Rashimia, and the baker's wife on some sea side town he couldn't remember the name of, he couldn't remember the girl's name either. There had been plenty of women for him to satiate his desires with, but he was set on his mission to find his love and he would not stop for anything, although he could no longer picture her face as clearly as he used to, and her voice had long gone from his mind, he would look forever if he had to. Blake often wondered what would happen when he found her, he fantasised about the day they would see each other and they would just *know* in their bones that they had been reunited, he could see how he would greet her. He dreamed she would be swept up in his arms and he would hold her tight and just listen to the beat of her heart, he hardly ever dared think of the possibility that she were dead and would only allow himself a moment each time, to really think on what had happened, what he could remember and try to let it lead him to her once more. Blake stared from the windows, seeing only the greyness of the fog and prayed for it to shift so he could admire this stronghold and find a way out, he wanted to see Fellyn's face at the reunion with her daughter. He realised he had not asked how old the child was, and why she had been left in the grass, she must be small to have been left sat in a patch of grass while her mother wandered away. He pondered this a while, and so many other aspects of the woman on the bed, so he was startled when she stirred and sat up.

Realising where she was, she looked over at Blake, her hair was tousled and her eyes shadowy from the night. Blake wondered whether she had been drooling in her sleep as she rubbed her hand along her chin. He smirked.

Fellyn saw his expression and asked him "What's wrong?"

"Nothing, dear maiden, but that you are entertaining to watch when asleep!" He chuckled.

Fellyn touched her hair self-consciously and used her fingers to sweep it to one side and pull the knots out. She rubbed her face with her hands, wishing to be nearer the pool once again to really bathe…but then again, with Blake around she wasn't sure she would dare anyway.

Blake offered her the small bundle of her own clothes she had brought up from the garden the day before, and she took them gratefully, her bluebell robe was crinkled and smelled of dampness since it hadn't fully dried when she had laid down to sleep. Without a word, he turned around the chair to face the door and sat in it, smilingly, imagining her body as she quietly changed back into the skirt she had sewn and her white shirt. She pulled back on her crinkled travelling cloak, but remembering their situation, placed it back on the bed and walked to the window to look for herself. Hearing her shift in position, Blake removed his hands from his face and turned to look at his companion, she was beautiful even in dirty clothes fit for a young lad!

"Fog again…have you tried the door yet?" Fellyn asked, not wishing to offend Blake, she felt incredibly self conscious after the night they had, and wished she had not poured out so much information to this stranger, but remembering his vow of protection, she looked up into his face and smiled. A touch of kindness would not hurt either of them.

"No, I rather thought it would be more obvious if it were opened!" Blake said teasingly.

Fellyn gave him an expression lacking amusement in return for his wit, and crossed the room to the door, turning the handle she was pleasantly surprised when it opened at her touch. The pair looked at each other, incredulous. Blake gestured for her to go first, then thought better of it.

"Wait, my lady, please…let me go first I will check the safety of the castle?" he said with a cheeky smile.

"What makes you think me incapable of judging the danger for myself, Blake?" Fellyn asked, retrieving her cloak and the bluebell robe from the bed and returning his boyish smile with her own graceful one, allowing herself to feel relief at their ability to leave what had become a stuffy prison for the night.

Regardless of her humour, Blake left the room first and she followed behind him, watching his cautious movement as he walked down the stairs, as he got to the bottom step he turned and yelled as if frightened by something. Fellyn had jumped herself, and moved back a few steps, stumbling on the fourth as she had been going backwards but the smirk on his face soon had her realising that she had fallen for

80

a silly joke. Blake was grinning at her "only joking, maiden, it is as void of humans as when we were last here!" he chuckled again and Fellyn glared at him.

"Oh very funny, Blake, frighten the only company you have!" she said, suppressing a laugh, he was really very enjoyable company and she was glad of his friendly companionship in the deserted castle.

"Dear maiden I am sorry to have scared you, but when moments of trouble test us, its always best to have a good laugh at something, it exercises the soul after all!" He said joyfully as he touched her arm and laughed again.

Fellyn smiled at him and rose from her half-seated position, finally she allowed herself a small giggle and they moved off together, Fellyn pondering whether he might be right, and tried to remember the last time she had actually laughed.

Blake took her arm in his, and they walked back to the garden, hoping for the fog to lift so that they might enjoy the day that never changed.

When they reached the garden, it was much the same as when they had last been there, Blake graciously gave Fellyn privacy to bathe in the pool and he came back to take a turn only when she called to him that she was dressed again. He, however, showed much the same modesty as before, which he took great pleasure in seeing as Fellyn's face turned a stunning shade of crimson when she blushed, and she busied herself with flowers once more.

Fellyn wandered the garden more than she had the last time, and came upon a wooden trunk which she opened to find small tools and a few bags of seeds, she smiled at the findings and took a few of the seeds and bulbs that she recognised; rosemary, garlic and sunflowers caught her eye and she took the curved blade of a hand held spade and went to work on the patch of unsown soil behind the low wall. She knelt to sow them, digging little rows for each type, ensuring that the sunflowers had the largest area to grow in, she did not understand the notion of time standing still, seeing as the flowers here bloomed and changed and bore fruit, time must be moving, surely?

Blake broke her concentration by admiring her work. "Lovely, and when exactly are you planning to harvest those?" he laughed, Fellyn stood, looking at her patch of sown seeds and smiled at them. She loved looking after her garden back in Tebel and the little moment of joy made her heart throb for what she was missing back in the village. Fellyn simply walked back to the end of the garden to where a few fruit trees stood proudly, she picked a handful of strange, slightly velvety golden fruit and several apples, took them back to where Blake was looking at her patch and they sat together on the low wall, eating their fill of fruit in comfortable silence. The velvety fruit was deliciously sweet, juicy and ripe, *it would make an excellent pie back home*, Fellyn thought to herself. She took the stones from the middle of the fruit, held out her hand for Blake's stones, and took them to the wooden box, *waste not*, she thought.

Blake dipped his sticky fingers into the pool and washed them, astonished at the clarity of the water even after they had bathed in it, Fellyn joined him once she had returned from the trunk, "Good idea!" she said and washed her own too. When they turned to look at the pretty garden again, each wondering what to do or where to go next, they saw that a small box was standing on the wooden trunk.

"Allow me." Said Blake guardedly, this place was curious at best, and he did not want Fellyn to see his reservations and fear. As he reached the small brown wooden case resting on the larger trunk, his hands were shaking, he opened the lid to find a large key inside. It was gilded with flourishing across the handle and was attached to a ring holding nothing else. He took the key from inside the box and moved back to Fellyn, showed her the key and the pair looked at it, wondering where it would fit.

"Should we move on? Find the door this unlocks?" Fellyn said quietly, aware that whoever was the bringer of the key, they would most likely be nearby. She suspected Nephi. But then, there really was nobody else to suspect here.

After deciding to turn a different way than Fellyn had gone towards the water arena, they followed a new corridor but tried each door with the key as they went. The key was large, so many of the doors were far too small to even need to try it. They worked their way in a large loop and then decided to take alternate turnings as to cover more of the castle to find the door which took the key. After a long time following the same paths to try different doors, turning back and going a different way, and finding themselves walking in circles, they came, somewhat accidentally, to a huge set of marble stairs headed upwards. Finding something besides the predictability of the castle corridors was a relief so they climbed confidently, sure that they were on to a new direction and a way out. Fellyn led the way up the stairs.

"I think this is moving out of the circular walkways, Blake!" she said, realising that they had been nowhere in the castle which held marble stairs, it felt as if they were headed towards an exit so she quickened her pace, hearing Blake match it with his own long strides. He caught up, flashed her a cheeky smile and started to overtake, she grinned back and they raced each other up the long marble stair case, Blake reaching the top first took a low bow to Fellyn who was panting a little.

"Ah, my lady, I am indebted to your kindness to allow me to win!" He said, with a wink, and raised himself back to standing. Fellyn shoved his arm out of her way playfully and faced the cross shaped intersection they had reached. Before them stood such a large door Fellyn thought that it must be as high as her hut back home...before the fire. She bristled at the memory, Blake was facing left and had frozen so Fellyn turned to see what he had seen.

Climbing through the line of arched windows were men, thick set men with spears in one hand and a dagger in the other, some had them in their teeth, they were pulling themselves into the chamber when one of them saw Blake and Fellyn and yelled to the others. A spear glanced past Blake's left ear, and hearing it whistle past her, Fellyn jumped into survival mode and grabbed his arm.

"Run, Blake!" she heaved at his arm and he moved backwards for a moment before turning and running, they were headed to the right, where she could see another line of windows, they were cornering themselves when a bunch of bandits had decided to raid the castle. They had no time to think of what they were doing but Fellyn looked out of a window, glad that she had bent over as a dagger ripped through the air where her head had just been, and collided with the top of the window and sat with a clatter at her feet. Fellyn grabbed the blade for herself and shoved it into Blake's hands, then she put her foot on to the ledge and clinging tight, she started to try and climb the window, Blake pulled her down.

"Don't be daft, lady, look!" He said and pointed to a door hidden in a crevice next to the windows, a small door. Blake dodged another spear and picked it up. Three of the bandits were dropping to the floor and headed their way, Blake grabbed the door and turned the handle, shoving Fellyn into its tiny frame before handing her the spear and following after her, pulling the door shut behind them. Darkness was all they could see, and Blake started using the spear to try and block the door from opening towards them, he managed to wedge the blade and the handle into some cracks in the brick, which held the door fast. They crawled through what seemed to be a small tunnel system until the floor fell from under them and they fell with a slam into a dingy room with very little light.

"Fellyn?" Blake said, realising that in the tight space of the tunnel he had nowhere to fall but on her, she was unconscious below his muscular body, so he pushed himself up, his hands either side of her bruised face. Whispering this time, so as not to attract any more unwanted attention, he said her name and stroked her thick black hair away from her face. She came around groggily, and saw his face above hers, whispering her name, she had hit her head hard and could feel the pounding in her head like a donkey kicking her repeatedly. She tried to sit up, but Blake moved her back to laying, he swept his cloak from around his neck and tucked it under her sore head, checking for injury while he did so, there was no blood, he relaxed a little. Fellyn was swimming in and out of consciousness and could only vaguely remember where she was and what her mind was trying to remember...

They were running, Althia by her side, they had slipped the rope from their feet while the guards slept and they had had time to remove the bindings from Althia's hands but one was stirring when they decided to run. They now felt the driving force of the snow in their faces as they ran as fast as their young legs could go. Althia was struggling again, she had not recovered from the last walk out here and was lagging behind a bit, Fellyn grabbed her arm with her own bound hands and pulled her along, they were running towards a dense patch of trees, desperate for cover and protection from the growling wind. The men were behind them, some had woken when Althia had cried out as she stumbled in the snow while running from the cave, the men had been disoriented but had been trying desperately to get their quarry back. The girls were blessed by the blizzard because as well as covering their tracks, it practically hid them from the view of the bandits but it was a curse also, it froze their faces and their bodies like the last fragile leaves in winter. The girls were running out of time to get to safety. As they neared the cover of trees they had been running to, Fellyn saw that a thick river was blocking their crossing to the forest and she stared at it bleakly, it was the dead of winter and the girls were small. She had decided to follow it a way, hoping for a way to cross when she heard the men shout nearby, they were not far if their voices could be heard over the driving wind. Fellyn grabbed Althia, "follow only where my feet go, unless you see it crack, okay?" she looked at her baby sister, who had not always been her closest friend, but whom Fellyn loved more than she did herself.

"Okay." Althia whispered.

Fellyn cautiously slid her foot onto the ice, testing the strength, it groaned under her weight but held her, she moved her other foot forwards and after a few tentative, slippery steps, felt safe to gesture Althia towards her.

"Take your time, it is dangerous sister." Fellyn said to the young girl. She was terrified.

As Althia took small tentative steps towards her sister, Fellyn moved away also, making sure her sister was only walking where she had tested the strength, men appeared from the covering of the snow, looking at the river which the girls had gotten half way across. They were much larger than the slight little girls and they hesitated, shouting obscenities at them, trying to distract them. Althia had turned to look at the men, looking back at her fear and in that moment her foot touched a patch of thinning ice, the water rippling below it caught Fellyn's eye and she grabbed her sisters hand to yank her away from the groaning crack under her. In that split second the ice cracked and the weight of both girls in Fellyn's hands pushed her down harder on the weakening ice. One of the smaller built men had started to try and reach them himself and as he stepped on the ice, a large crack formed which broke Fellyn's foothold, shoving her sister away from the crack, almost to the other side of the river, she shouted "RUN!" before the ice gave way and she slipped under its frozen trap. Blinding pain and sharp daggers ripped at her skin but she couldn't scream for the water and ice suffocating her face, the current had pushed her under the ice to a further point and as she pushed against it herself to break free, she saw a delicate little hand appear on the other side. Althia. The precious little hand was jolted away suddenly and Althia was gone as Fellyn felt her lungs fill with fire and ice, and she slipped into oblivion.

Chapter 9 – The Temple

" Be thou my vision, O Lord of my heart

Naught be all else to me save that thou art

Thou my best thought by day or by night

Waking or sleeping thy presence my light.

Be thou my battleshield, sword for the fight

Be thou my dignity, thou my delight

Thou my soul's shelter, thou my high tower

Raise thou me heavenward, O power of my power.

High King of heaven, after victory won

May I reach heaven's joys, O bright heaven's sun

Heart of my own heart, whatever befall

Still be my vision, O ruler of all."

(Dallan Forgaill 1905)

Fellyn's eyes opened with a snap, and she stared at the arms cradled around her. Her mind calm from the song she had heard in her dream.

She was ice cold from the stone floor but his body was as warm as when laying by a roaring fire, comforting and strong. She could hear his heavy breathing as he slept holding her head and shoulders, his body curled around her own so she was covered by his warmth yet the cold stone beneath them was chilling them through. Fellyn was very aware that this man holding her was not her husband, but as the fear coursed through her veins again, remembering the past she had dreamed, and their flight through the castle, Fellyn was glad of Blake and the security he was offering. She gently raised her hand and tenderly stroked a long cut which traced the muscle on the back of his arm, it was inflamed and needed cleaning, but for the lack of light in wherever they rested, she could see no way to wash him here. She did not want to wake him, for it was comforting hearing him sleep and being held was remarkably comfortable. She also knew that when Blake awoke he would feel obliged to move his arms, and she rather hoped that would not happen.

Suddenly filled with a pang of guilt for her marriage bed, or lack of, she turned her body in his arms, wincing as she did so and gently peeled herself from his strong embrace. He roused at the movement, and she pulled away quicker so he would not know of her comfort at his actions as they slept. Blake sat up and looked at her with a sleepy smile.

"How do you feel, maiden?" He asked, groggily.

"My head and back are terribly sore, but otherwise I am unhurt, and you?" Fellyn asked, deciding not to mention their sleeping arrangements.

"Better rested for the company" Blake winked at her, and pushed himself to his feet. So all hope of leaving the subject to rest was shattered. "Now, maiden, while you were sleeping I discovered that we are in fact in a prison. I cannot see our entry point which leads me to think it was a successfully secret means of escaping this place, but we are most likely safest here since that exit would take us uphill back to those men." Blake spoke to her, as if their experiences were normal rather than horrifying.

"Do we have water?" Fellyn asked, she was parched and longed for the cool pond in her little garden. Thinking of its delicious spring only made her desire worse and she closed her eyes to imagine the clear water of the pretty pond. Her mind flicked back to the wineskin strapped to Luca's back and she scowled at her irritation that she had no water when usually she kept a full supply at all times.

"No, my sweet lady, we have nothing but our cloaks, weapons and the key with us." Blake answered regretfully, inspiration struck and he decided to try the lock with the key, it was a long shot but might pay off. So hurrying to the lock he pulled out the key and tried it but the key would not fit into the smaller lock and dejected, Blake sat once more. He had settled himself close behind Fellyn and gently pulled her shoulders so she was leaning with her back against him. Fellyn did not object, thirst and pain were clouding her judgement so she once more fell into his lap and allowed herself to relax. His hands rubbed small circles over her back and shoulders like she had once done for animals at Tehya's when they were injured, she turned and smiled at Blake wanting to ask him where he had learned to do that too.

"How old is your daughter, Fellyn?" Blake whispered, breaking Fellyn's concentration before she had a chance to ask.

"She is but three months of age." Fellyn smiled thinking of her sweet baby girl. "She is such a happy baby, always full of smiles and so easy going, she likes to ride along when I hunt or...travel." She was lost in her thoughts, her heart aching for the darling child she was missing so much.

Blake stroked her hair and said "we will find her, Fellyn, we shall leave this place and find her I am sure of it."

"I wish I were as confident as that, I fear all the worst things are happening to her and I fear for myself if I lose her." Turning to face

Blake, but then leaning away to a safer distance she said "I cannot lose the only good thing in my life, Blake." Her eyes welled up and refusing to succumb to her emotions, she blinked the tears away and pushed herself to standing.

A faint amount of light was coming through the balistraria window and Fellyn watched the dancing dust floating in the slim ray of sunlight that fell on the floor at Blake's feet. Writing was slightly visible where the beam fell, and she bent down quickly, scrubbing at the dusty flag stones to clear the dirt away.

Fellyn read the words to herself, but confused by their meaning she then read it aloud for Blake to hear too.

"Until I am measured

I am not known,

Yet how you miss me

When I have flown."

Blake looked at the riddle himself, then back up at Fellyn. "Well what does that mean?"

"I do not know." Fellyn shrugged. "Perhaps we must solve it to get out?" There could be no other reason, unless it were simply the mad writings of a prisoner from long ago.

They sat, running through what it was possible to measure, from land, material, height, weight and so on, going around and around until they were desperately frustrated.

Bored and irritated by the riddle, Blake was beginning to get restless, he was stood with his back to the wall right beside the balistraria as Fellyn stood in front of the window staring out into the foggy day outside. She really was rather stunning, with her black hair tied loosely in a bun at the base of her neck, ruffled from sleeping on a floor. Her face which was drawn in concentration was flawless. Blake noticed a small mark behind her ear, curiously in the shape of a fish, he felt himself drawn to her and felt the need to touch her fair skin.

"What flies...birds can fly, perhaps measure a bird? No...that makes no sense at all. Perhaps a dragon...but why would it be missed?" Fellyn was muttering to herself.

"How about the measure of a man, maiden?" Blake winked at her and as she had ignored him, he moved closer and wrapped his arms around her waist in a slightly mocking attempt to kiss her, making light of his attraction to her and their situation. He had not been planning to kiss Fellyn really, but in the moment she had looked so inviting in that sliver of sunlight that he could not have resisted trying.

Fellyn felt her body move towards Blake as he tugged at her hips and his mouth met hers in what he obviously intended to be a gesture of romance, but Fellyn was insulted and felt violated for his insolence. She shoved him away with all her strength and put her hand to her lips, the taste of him still on her and she bit back at the attempt to covet her virtue.

"Blake, I am no harlot but a married woman!" She half shouted, furious at him for attempting such a thing, in such a place with no hint of consent on her part. He was offended by her refusal and his ego had been bruised, but it was not the first time a woman had done so at his advances.

Stifling a laugh, Blake replied "no, maiden, I am sorry but you are beautiful and this is such a lonely place as to make a man wish to spend his final hours happy." He flashed her his cheeky smile which she did not return.

"Final hours? We aren't sentenced to..." Fellyn broke off mid thought, for another had taken over her mind. Hours could fly when you were happy and would be missed... "Time, Blake, the answer is time!"

The sound of clapping drowned out her discovering the riddle's answer and made the suddenly euphoric moment end abruptly. Nephi was applauding them slowly, walking towards them on the other side of the bars to the prison. "How entertaining you both are!" Nephi stopped clapping and grinned.

"Nephi, where have you been? Will you let us out?" Fellyn asked, crossing to the door of the cell and leaning against the cold bars with both hands.

"I can, when I hear your answer to the riddle." Nephi replied.

Fellyn had assumed he had heard her say the answer but she repeated it to him, too happy to see Nephi and in the knowledge that he would release them to question why he had come if not for the answered riddle.

"Correct!" Nephi cried, he raised his hands heavenward and the doors snapped open at once, swinging on their hinges towards Fellyn and Blake, they walked through the doors towards Nephi who was leaning against the wall, a smile playing on his blue lips.

"Come, young ones, you have been summoned." Nephi said excitedly.

Blake looked at Fellyn, as confused as the expression she returned. "By whom?" Blake questioned.

Nephi's returning smile was not comforting in place of an explanation.

Nephi had led them through the maze-like castle and into a section they had not explored at all, nor even been close to. He ascended several flights of stairs, led them through another two courtyards which were not the same garden Fellyn had visited and found so comforting. A dread was filling her, reminiscent of the fear she associated with being chastised by Tehya as a child, or having been given a warning by an older man of Tebel who had been angry with her for picking fruit from his private trees. Blake was less concerned, he was looking forward to an opportunity to have a little talk with Nephi about the goings on here, starting with his lack of memory about how he ended up drowning in a water arena.

They came to a sudden stop outside of a building separate from the castle itself, built within a very large courtyard like the walls of the castle were protecting this smaller citadel. Looking to Nephi for confirmation, and getting a small nod of the head in response, Blake walked forwards up the wide steps to the large door, totally magnetised by the place and his desire to go inside ruling his feet. Fellyn walked as to follow Blake's progress, but Nephi held his arm out to block her path, she stopped short of touching him and he flinched away from her, but he shook his head. "He requested each of you alone." Nephi said.

Fellyn didn't question him, but she shook her head in irritation as she settled herself gently on the luscious grass of the courtyard. She sat for a while, deep in thought, before she asked Nephi in a hushed voice "why did you leave me alone in the castle?"

Nephi faced her and looked into her deep brown eyes full of questions and concern, "because you needed to find your truth, something that I could not help you to see, it is for Him to give enlightenment." Nephi turned his back on the girl. He sat staring up at the sun unblinking, and Fellyn suddenly realised that there was a distinct lack of fog, so asked the question she had been longing to know of Nephi.

"Time...is it really still while I am here? Is Etana still safe at the gates with Luca?" She rose to standing, sheer desperation pulling her fragile heart beyond its limits. She waited to hear whether she could relax and endure long enough for Nephi's sick game of traps and trials to end to be allowed home to her daughter.

Nephi did not answer her, but instead said with his back still facing the girl "He calls you in now. You must go." And as Fellyn rose up the steps herself to meet her captor she turned back to Nephi, he was watching her with intrigue and a smile.

"Has this all been a game, Nephi? This place, it seems…cruel." Fellyn's tone was full of the hurt she had felt here, the pain of reliving her past and being thrown into the agony of realising what loss could do to a person.

"My dear girl, nothing here is ever what your human mind sees. You see only what is before your eyes, but there is more that you could not comprehend that makes this place what it truly is. If you need the truth, you must enter the Temple." Nephi had stepped up so that he stood only just below Fellyn, they stared each other down and Fellyn could not shake the feeling that she had known his face before. She had been so blinded by fear that it had not occurred to her back when they had met. *Ice* she thought, *through the ice.*

She sighed and turned to rise up the large steps but before she reached the top, Fellyn looked back for Nephi. She wanted to thank the ethereal, blue-tinged stranger who had helped her through the underpass so little time and yet so long ago, but he had gone.

When Fellyn reached the door and opened it, Blake crossed her mind and she wondered if he were still inside. However, when she stepped over the threshold of the temple, she felt the overwhelming power it embodied and her whole being reacted to its presence. She doubled over, completely losing control of her body's decision and was on her knees, finding herself fearfully and joyously prostrate. She wept. Uncontrollably and unashamedly, her whole body being wracked by the heart-breaking fears, hurts, betrayals and judgement she had faced in her short time. Her mind was totally and completely clear of reasons for her emotion, she simply wept before the altar and in His goodness, He consoled her soul.

After a lifetime of regret and damage had been refined from her heart, she felt Him call her to stand. She did so, incapable of speech and so unworthy of it even if she could have chosen to, she simply waited on Him.

A figure was before her, human in stature but glowing bright like the watery sunshine of a winter morning, flowing hair of gold and a robe of liquid light around its frame. It spoke with authority and with power, speaking a message old as time.

"Now saith the LORD that created thee, and He that formed thee, Fear not: for I have redeemed thee, I have called thee by thy name; thou art mine. He hath saved thee from the hand of them that despised you, and redeemed you from the hand of your enemy. Saith the Lord that the waters covered your enemies: there was not one of them left. I, the Lord, have ransomed thee from the power of the grave; I redeem thee from death. In all your affliction I AM afflicted, in love and in pity I have redeemed thee; and I will love thee for all of the days in Thine hand."

Flooded by purifying water in her very soul and still unable to look to the altar at which she stood, Fellyn breathed deeply and felt her eyes drawn to the figure in gold. She found her heart and mouth filled with song

"Rob tu mo bhoile,

a Comdi cride.

Ni ni nech aile,

acht ri secht nime ..."

As she was singing in strange tongue not her own, she felt the words completely consume her heart and she sang louder hearing a choir of voices from her mouth and yet from all around her.

Utterly ablaze with the emotion in the room, and rejuvenated by the spirit in the temple, she found herself face down in cool grass at dusk. The place felt dim compared to the Temple, and she wished she had gotten a better look at the gold figure and the origin of the light in such huge amounts. A storm was coming in just as when she was last here...and she suddenly heard a baby's cry. *Etana!*

Fellyn felt her body stand and as relief and rejoice took over her heart she ran to her tiny bundle, still wrapped in the carrying cloth she had bound to her chest, Luca lying faithfully by the side of the bundle, firewood and bags strapped to her strong body and her tail wagging madly. Fellyn drew her tiny daughter into her arms and as close to her heart as she could physically manage, she cradled the baby for a long time, throwing the carrying cloth over her shoulder and welcoming the child to her and finding sweet release in feeding her addiction to this delightful child.

Her eyes pouring and her heart overflowing, Fellyn laughed into the growing dark and felt a hand on her shoulder. Blake was standing behind her, hands holding two loaves of the delicious bread she had eaten with Nephi and a large goblet also. He was smiling like he had been drinking the sumptuous wine and glowing like a man in love. They laughed and ate together then drank the sweet nectar of the goblet, and without words, Fellyn rose to her feet holding Etana tightly. Blake took the carrying cloth from her and wound it around

96

her back and shoulders tightly as she slipped Etana safely back against her warm body. They stood together and realised they had been released from their prison; but a prison it no longer seemed. Rather, a fire of refinement and a refuge. How strange it seemed to be fond of such a place after so much had happened. Blake took a look around them both, and taking charge of their direction he headed out North West with Fellyn close to his side, unwittingly walking towards the very thing from which she had run.

Chapter 10 – Fear and Love

He sat staring into the flickering light of the fire and thought of his wife. He allowed his mind to wander to her delicate hips which she used so impressively for balancing a basket of cloth or firewood and to balance Etana while she worked around the house. He thought of his hands upon those fine hips in their early days of courting when touching her was as tantalising as holding fresh meat to a dog's nose. The first time he had held her hips was when he had been teaching her to use his bow, she had been struggling to balance when releasing the arrow to flight and he had asked her to move her legs further apart and had placed his hands on her firmly to ask her to stand strong in her stance. He looked down at his hands and smiled at the memory of how she had blushed the colour of the roses around them, and how her eyes had danced when instead of moving away as a valiant tutor would have, he allowed them to remain rested on her body and waited for her to initiate their removal. He had kicked those hips too since then...

He missed her hands also, hands which were capable of kneading dough for hours, scrubbing a floor until they were red raw and of beating the dust from their rugs. They were also capable of soothing an infant into soft sleep and of causing him the most unbearable desire with only a brush of her fingertips. Fingertips that he had kissed tenderly as young lovers and which would tenderly sweep the hair from his eyes while he worked, fingers he had crushed with his own angry hands.

His hands had caused pain to his wife, caused her heart to crumble instead of open to him and caused her to become a fearful and quiet companion instead of the fiery and passionate woman she had been to him. He had broken her wings and then had watched her try to run from him many times, and now she had, Jared had no idea how he would ever find and bring Fellyn home. Nor how he would embalm his wild temper and relieve Fellyn of the burden his beatings had left her with. The memory of seeing her using a poultice to cover her bruised face, and the way she had flinched when he had touched her shoulder in an attempt to apologise made his eyes burn with the need to cry and allowed him to see what had been her reason to leave Tebel. He could see that she had never intended to shame him by telling anyone and he could see that all of the reasons he used to spend his time with Rhia were wrong. He had told himself it was because Rhia was everything Fellyn was not, but that was not true, Fellyn had been like Rhia once but it felt like so long ago that he had forgotten her in place of the broken dove he had created. He felt the guilt entwine his body and mind and felt unclean for the thoughts he had entertained about Rhia. He could see now that what he had done to Fellyn would be what would happen to Rhia after a marriage to him, and that for all the bad he had thought about Cassius for his lust not love for Rhia was ridiculous in place of the alternative of a broken wife. *What an enormous burden a woman must take upon herself in marriage if all men were like himself and Cassius*, he thought.

Tehya peered through the leaves of the tree she was sat in. A barn owl had perched just below her and was eyeing her with loathing, she had leaned against the hollow of the tree which this feathery friend apparently wanted to sit in. Tehya huffed, it had taken her far too long to get in that tree and then get comfortable so she had no plans whatsoever to move any time soon. Also she had yet to figure out her route down again so her options were distinctly limited anyway. As if reading her expression or her mind, the owl flew off in search of another branch, or perhaps some dinner. Tehya concentrated on Jared again, he had been following the path towards the mountains in a fairly linear route, with some exceptions that is, such as following his own boot print around in a circle for a half a day thinking it had been

Fellyn, whose feet were rather smaller than his own. Tehya had found that particularly amusing.

Jared's face was furrowed and tears marked a path from his sleep deprived eyes to his strong chin. He was full of remorse now and Tehya raised her own chin, feeling joy at seeing the revelation that this journey was allowing him. It was about time he saw the error of his ways, fear and love were not so separate after all. Knowing now that Jared was on the right track, and that if she continued steering him that he was likely to see her hand in it eventually, she decided to head home come morning. Jared was unlikely to turn back from the remorse he was showing now that it was plain to his eyes, and Fellyn had shown the courage to get out once, it was likely she could handle him now if she were unhappy.

Blake was sitting on a log, in front of the fire he had made for them with two large fish wrapped in leaves and speared by a thin branch held out over the flames to cook. Fellyn had smothered the fish in an aromatic herb and his taste buds were tingling as the smell of the fish sent his growling belly into knots waiting for the food. Blake was ravenous, he hadn't eaten well in days, missing the good food he would often find in the home of some kindly family, especially of a kindly woman he would purposefully befriend. Women loved Blake's humour and looks, he was not a stranger to meeting a nice girl working in an inn, and wooing her for the night to ensure himself a good meal and a cosy bed for the night, not to mention the warm body in the bed with him.

He shook his head, thinking that he could never again take a woman that way since his experience in the Temple. He remembered it with all the hazy qualities that one sees when trying to call to mind a wonderful dream. He thought of the chorus singing behind him from where, he could not tell. He cast his mind back to the figure in gold that had heralded his Lord's forgiveness for Blake's past and cleansing from all wrongs. Blake's spine tingled in thinking of the overwhelming presence in that place and how good it had been.

He looked up from his thoughts to see Fellyn busying herself with piles of leaves under the low falling branches of the tree she had chosen to sleep next to. Luca was lapping at the stream to their left, letting her long fur fall into the water and shaking it occasionally. Blake liked the dog, it was pleasant to see the way Fellyn and Luca had a sort of unspoken understanding, she spoke to Luca like a human and the dog was as obedient as if she understood the girl's words. The dog would watch over Etana when Fellyn had hunted for them, catching the fish and collecting berries and fruit.

Blake was an efficient forager himself, having been a traveller for so long it was second nature for him to be on the hunt for food constantly, but Fellyn was as expert at it as if she too had always been a traveller. She and the dog had taken down a hare from what he had laughingly said to be an impossible distance. They were as refined as a couple of long standing soldiers and as trusting of each other as the best of friends. Blake watched Etana kick her tiny legs around in the patch of leaves that Fellyn had laid down for her, cooing and chirping as she looked at her own tiny fingers, an expression on her face showing her amazement at finding such treasure. Blake chuckled and moved over to the baby, enchanted by her beautiful eyes and rosebud mouth. Her high little voice trilled when his face registered in her view, she kicked her legs harder as if running in the air and flung her arms out, grinning at him in-between chirpy sounds, Blake was utterly adoring of little Etana, she had him completely at her beck and call, just like her mother!

Fellyn smiled at the sight of Blake with her baby, his strong finger being wrapped by her tiny fist, and his eyes enchanted by her smile. It was strange for her to see a man take such loving interest in a child so small, the men of Tebel were unmoved by the babies in the village, preferring to leave it until the children were grown enough to learn a trade then they were happy to speak and play with them. It had always confused Fellyn, as a sort of male pride gesture, but this seemed utterly natural to her and she was enjoying watching them immensely.

Fellyn finished sorting their beds of leaves, she had put Blake's bed once again rather far from her own, feeling self conscious about the kiss at the castle, and ashamed that she had thought of him often since leaving. Also it was awkward for her to feed Etana when Blake was there, she was reserved about revealing herself when feeding so had been using their carrying cloth to cover herself which was all well until Etana's strong little legs kicked the cloth away leaving Fellyn with one hand cradling the baby, the other trying to replace the fallen cloth and not enough hands to hold Etana's hands and legs from kicking it away again.

Fellyn shook the thought of her embarrassment away and went to where Luca was paddling in the water and filled the wineskin which had been strapped to the dog during her time in the castle, she drank of it and re-filled it again. She gracefully walked to where Blake was making Etana giggle, and very conscious of holding herself well and sucking in her stomach, she handed Blake the wineskin and smiled at him. Etana recognised her mother's face and started wriggling furiously, letting out an excited squeal of delight so Fellyn scooped the baby into her arms and spun around holding her in tight, which made Etana squeal again. When Fellyn stopped spinning, she too was laughing. She saw Blake's eyes on her, his lips moist from the water and his smile comfortable he moved in towards them, and took her right hand in his left, then wrapped his right arm around her left arm cradling Etana and he led them in a dance around the camp fire. They were spinning around in graceful circles, Etana squeaking between them, their laughter contagious. They slowed to a stand still, Fellyn's head buzzing with joy at their dance, her heart full of laughter and she felt his hand move higher up her left arm, and his other down to her hip pulling her in closer to him. She did not move from his hold, but stared into his blue tinged eyes and was captivated. He leaned in closer to her and she readied herself for a kiss she assumed was coming, but with no intention of stopping him this time.

Instead, he bent his head forward and planted a gentle kiss on Etana's downy head and smiled at her responding chirp, then straightened up and pulled Fellyn's free hand to his lips and put the kiss which she had wanted to embrace with her own on to her fingers instead, as the gentleman she had not known he would be. Blake stepped away again slowly, releasing his tender hold of the girls and made a little bow flourishing his hand as if removing a hat, then with that easy smile on his lips again he moved back to the fire to take the fish from their spears and check them.

"Dinner is served, maiden!" he said without turning to where Fellyn still stood, abandoned in the moment she had been lost in, fighting to control the animal Blake had awakened inside her. She blinked herself out of the moment, bounced Etana on her hip and went to settle by the fire with Blake, sitting further away than was really necessary but completely determined not to give in and feed the animal's desire. Guilt rushed through her as she thought again of Jared, no matter his actions against her, she could not ever betray him.

Blake handed her a fish, the larger of the two and their fingers brushed as she took it, Fellyn's stomach somersaulted and she blushed and mumbled her thanks then busied herself with her fish until it was gone entirely except for the head, tail and splintery bones. Blake was licking his fingers clean of the oily juices, which Fellyn definitely did not need to see. She hurried to collect all of the fish left and took it to where Luca had laid herself on the leaves where Fellyn would sleep later, she encouraged Luca to a spot further from the beds and ruffled her thick long fur as she wolfed down the leftovers. The dog licked her long snout clean and set herself back on the bed to clean her paws, "we ought to call it a night too." Fellyn said, not daring herself to look at Blake.

"As you wish, my lady." Blake whispered back, he stood and moved towards her, kissed the top of her head affectionately and then stroked Etana's hair. He doused the fire with water and stepped on it hard to put it out, secretly hoping that nobody was close enough to see the smoke in the twilight.

103

Fellyn had snuggled herself into her leafy bed, her travelling cloak over her with Etana cuddled up to her chest, Luca the other side of the baby keeping the pair warm. When Blake was settled himself, he quietly asked "Fellyn, where are you going now?"

There was a long silence while Fellyn pondered her answer, "to find where I belong, I suppose." She said, hoping he would not hear the pain in her voice.

"Are you planning to ever return to him?" Blake questioned, knowing which answer he would prefer.

"I don't know what to do, he is my husband and I must do my best for our marriage...I made vows to him and I cannot forget them...But I would die before I allow Etana to be raised in a dangerous home so for now I think we just need to...keep on moving." Fellyn had felt her determination to be safe for her baby's sake, but until she stated it aloud had not realised that her marriage was second in that order. She was utterly confused about her path, she wanted to be a good and honest wife but she could not stay where Etana was unsafe.

"Maiden, are we to travel together somewhere in particular? I am headed home to my village, it has been years since seeing my dear family so it would be pleasant to see them before I set off again. Would you come with me? I can protect you..." Blake asked, not wishing to inculpate that she could not care for herself.

Fellyn thought for a long time again and Blake wondered if she had fallen asleep but she whispered "yes...I would like to travel with you a while, thank you."

"Well, fair maiden, now that we know our heading, let us sleep and hope for a bright tomorrow!" He said happily and smiled as he drifted to sleep.

Seven men stumbled from the castle walls, not one of them sure exactly how they had escaped the wall of water that had rushed at them as they fled through the high gates. Garreck looked at the men around him and checked his scabbard for the large dagger at his waist. His weapon firmly in place, he checked his men. A few of them were missing their own daggers and two their spears. He walked to where Slint stood with a dagger safely at his waist and a spear in hand and took the large weapon for himself, Slint opened his fingers begrudgingly and allowed the more experienced man to take it from him.

"Make sure you each have a weapon." Garreck barked at them. A confused scuffle broke out as men argued about what they each carried and who deserved the best of them. "Share, boys, or I'll do it for you!" Garreck sneered, and they moved out into the forest away from the South West gate.

On the North West path from Tebel, Jared slept. His fire still ablaze in an unwitting invitation to the men a few miles from his camp. Tehya had squirreled a handful of raspberries from a bush and had been eating them as she walked. She had gotten herself out of the tree and was walking quietly back along the path they took, heading back to a clump of thick bushes she had planned to settle in for the night, something was making her uneasy but she could not place quite why. As she moved further from Jared, she could hear voices, her heart froze, and then resumed thumping audibly. She looked around her for a place to hide but she was following the thinner path as it was dark with only a waning moon for light so there was no tree to climb easily for her weak and tired body. There were no thick bushes here just sparsely dotted saplings, Tehya saw a thicker tree trunk and hurried to it, hiding in its shadow facing away from the path hoping that in the darkness they would not see her.

She waited there hearing her heart bang forcefully for what seemed an eternity when several men, she could not tell how many, crossed her view. They were heavy set and armed with spears and daggers, shoving each other roughly and laughing amongst themselves. They followed the path she had been on and she quietly thanked God for the lack of rain today meaning the ground had been hard enough not to leave prints behind her. After they had moved far enough away that she would consider moving from her spot into the heavier trees, one stopped, turned and sniffed hard. Tehya looked at her hand clutching the berries and damned them for their tart scent. All of them hurried their pace, moving like smoke through the trees, slashing branches and ripping roots up in search of its source. Tehya could not tell if they were hungry and searching for food, or for the one who had been eating fruit nearby.

Tehya backed slowly from the shade and tried to run for a bush close to her but one of the men saw her as a foot disappeared behind it, he charged her way and she tried to run but her body was old and frail. He grasped her arm and twisted, yanking her roughly to the ground, she lay writhing in pain assuming her arm was broken by the force he had used and the snap she had felt. He stamped his foot down hard on her arm and the agony shot through her body causing her to cry out in pain. A wave of nausea swept over her body and she fought to keep the berries from reappearing. Tehya cried out again, hopefully Jared would hear her and run away from the sound, she hoped he was no hero for he stood no chance here. The men gathered around her and their faces swam in and out of her blurred view as her brain tried to block out the agony and allow her sweet release. Two pairs of hands yanked her upwards and threw her to sitting with her back to the tree she had run from, her unsafe hiding space. A large dirty blonde haired man crouched in front of her, he tilted his head mockingly and laughed in her face.

"Looky looky lads, it's the hag of the village! Fancy a night with us madam, I bet it's been a while since you 'ad male company!" Their raucous laughter shattered the quiet in the forest. Tehya said nothing but hung her head so as not to give him the satisfaction of her concentration. Irritated by her insubordination he threw his fist hard into her face, blood streamed from her nose and she felt a tooth rattle around on her tongue, her head pounding under the weight of his hand's force. Tehya turned her head to the man, and spitting blood as she spoke said "The Lord will be your judge and jury, so think hard about how you treat me." They laughed again and as her words fuelled the fire, one shouted "'ave 'er, Garrek!"

A spear plunged into Tehya's ribcage, ripping through her like mere paper. Her world jolted as he tore it out of her again and as she slipped in and out of consciousness, agony a fire all over her body, Garrek used his fingers to shove the wound, laughing and defiling her as the Lord carried her home on a wave of beautiful peace.

Chapter 11 – Controlling Factors

Fellyn saw Tehya's screaming mouth like a door to hell, the men from the castle stabbing her frail body and using their hands inside of her to pull the wound open, ripping her apart like pulling petals from a closed rose. She saw them tear her clothes from her bleeding and ravaged skin, Tehya's eyes blank and staring, and their predatory faces distort as they raped her open wound and her naked femininity. Fellyn saw flashes of each defiling her very being and unashamedly committing a sin as old and as dark as the world around her. The larger of the men, with the scar across his nose, then took his dagger and ripped through Tehya's body, removing her limb from limb until it was no longer Tehya there but a broken shell of a corpse. That man's face swam into Fellyn's mind, distorting with monstrousness, horns and blazing red eyes, his laughter fuelled a hatred strong enough to murder though Fellyn's heart, she woke to find her eyes streaming tears and a scream on her lips waiting to be released.

The images she had seen had been so real to her yet she knew it was simply a dream, a terrifying and haunting image of the men she herself had escaped. Fellyn dared not move for the infant cradled at her breast and the sound of Blake's breathing but in that moment she longed to have his firm arms cradling her too, for safety and assuring her that he was not leaving her alone. Ironic how she could feel more vulnerable with him than she ever had when alone, as if the thought of

108

being alone after being with him was worse than never having met him. Fellyn could not fall asleep, she could still feel the pain of Tehya inside her and was too frightened to sleep. She watched over the camp from her bed of leaves, pins and needles in the arms that cuddled Etana close, Luca lifted her head and whimpered a little, licking the air and then returning her head to the ground.

"Hush, Luca." Fellyn comforted, assuring herself as much as the dog of their safety. But it was all she could do to stay in place until dawn began to approach, she sleepily fed Etana her fill of milk, noticing that she no longer had as much of it as she had before and worried for Etana that she was not getting enough nutrition. Fellyn quietly roused Blake, shaking his shoulder and asking him to move on for she was concerned that they had been here too long. His pale eyes looked at her concern and the circles shadowing her brown eyes, he saw how little sleep she must have had and stroked the hair from her face. He sat up and cradled her face in his warm hand.

"Why so scared maiden? Did you hear something?" he asked, his face and tone as serious as she; waiting for her answer, but she simply shook her head and handed him the wineskin for a drink. They both drank well and Fellyn knelt by the stream to ensure the container was brimming with water. Blake had scattered the ashes and branches of the fire and covered it with their leaf beds, hiding that there had been a camp here at all as best he could. Fellyn tied Etana to her, tighter than usual, and they all moved out into the woods again, heading closer to the mountains and feeling the air grow cooler around them as the day passed by.

As they moved through the thinning trees, closer to the foot of the mountain range, conversation was fairly slim. Blake chatted as usual about all sorts of things such as places he had seen and what he had liked about them, or people he had met. Blake had hundreds of amusing stories to share with Fellyn. He talked of being thrown overboard from a ship heading away from Xandia and having to swim

all the way back again purely due to a disagreement with the
quartermaster over the right to sleep when he felt like it. Blake was
laughing as he described the scene.

"...You should have seen his face when I refused to mop the deck
as punishment, I mean, I was only hitching a lift and had paid them in
salted game birds so it wasn't as if I were riding free and being lazy!
Anyway, I said to him that I'd sleep until sundown and all night again
if I so wished and he said 'well, sonny, if you're plannin' on takin' to
yer bed all day you better have a lassy in there to share with us all!' and
I laughed out loud at this, he didn't like that much I can tell you, and
then I said 'no, there's no girl there so unless you're offering me your
own company in there I'll request you leave me be!' he had me ordered
to be whipped and sent overboard but I told the officer I'd give him
my bottle of rum if he had me thrown overboard minus the whipping!
I never did see outside of Xandia but lucky for me and my swimming
we hadn't made it too far around the Island before heading out into
the open sea!" Blake finished, still laughing at his memories but Fellyn
was lost in her own and had been nodding along with his words
without really hearing him.

Blake pulled her to a stop gently, "hey, maiden, what's gotten into
you today? You look like you've seen a ghost, sour faced since
morning and half asleep. You didn't even touch the berries I found
us." Fellyn's head drooped a little, she could not explain why she felt
so down and so weak today but she could not shake off the images of
Tehya from her dreams, they haunted her every thought and made her
feel sick.

Fellyn shook her head at Blake's questions and said "I can't explain
it, Blake, I just feel like something awful has happened."

To her surprise, Blake laughed, "maiden is this about last night? I
didn't mean to be forceful with you again I did hear you back at the
castle, and I am changed by that temple." Blake put one hand over his
heart and smiled at her with genuine eyes. "I am sorry if that's what
you thought but it wasn't like that, I was just so happy to be with both

of you last night and its not as if we have enough fun!" He tilted her chin up again but seeing her face was downcast regardless, he released her and stood up straight.

"No, Blake, last night was…fun and I did not feel at all like you were trying anything with me." Fellyn huffed a little and started walking, Luca trotted at her faster pace.

Blake caught up to Fellyn, "well, what is bothering you maiden?" He asked, a frown wrinkling his handsome features.

"I dreamed that Tehya, who is my mother for all intents and purposes, was murdered and…defiled…" Fellyn winced, remembering the awful images. "It sickened me greatly and I am frightened that it could be true. I have never had such a vivid dream, Blake, like I was there watching it all." Fellyn was shaking at the memory of Tehya's broken body.

"It was a dream maiden." Blake said softly, pulling her a touch closer to himself, intending to comfort her for his heart was breaking at her pain. He thought better of embracing her at the last moment, not wanting to offend her again. "Just a bad dream and no wonder since you're frightened anyway." He put his arm around her shoulder in a comfortable, friendly gesture and Fellyn leaned her head on him as they walked onwards. They talked of trivial things and of different areas of the land. Blake talked of the sea ports and the tendencies of men to drink. He spoke of the swamp lands and the pretty women there who wore no boots but went barefoot in the marshes, pulling weeds to stew for supper.

Fellyn listened while they trudged through the woods, the land under their feet changing to become less flat than that of Tebel, small hills rocked the area and gave them challenges to move around or over. Fellyn was used to seeing an abundance of game, but here she was seeing more of the smaller, rarer birds than game, less to hunt but more beautiful to observe. Etana chirped her little responses to the bird calls, kicking her legs furiously as if she wanted to roam the land.

While her growing mind and strengthening body were lovely for Fellyn
to see, it meant that the bundle was causing her neck to tighten and
become less comfortable.

"Let me take her a while." Blake asked, seeing Fellyn rubbing her
neck when they had stopped for a rest at around midday. Her back was
still sore from her fall in the castle and she was not used to the
growing weight of her daughter, at least that was reassurance enough
that Etana was feeding well.

Fellyn nodded, feeling the tug of her heart as she agreed to let
Blake share responsibility, and stopping her mind wondering what
would happen were they separated at all, she silently told herself not to
let them wander at all and only let Blake take her for a short time.

Blake came to where Fellyn had sat to rest, he knelt behind her to
untie the material which held Etana in place. Once finished, Blake
stood and tied the cloth around his own body as he had seen Fellyn do
it, but the material sagged wrong and seemed to be lopsided, he looked
at Fellyn who was suppressing a laugh.

"This seems to be harder than it looks, maiden!" Blake laughed.
Fellyn flipped Etana over and laid her with a curled Luca in the grass,
she stood and took the material ends from Blake, she turned him
around and gently pulled and looped the material, crossing it here and
there to form the carrier sections. She pulled him slowly to face her
and brought the material to the front to tie it in place. "Here, I can..."
Blake said quietly, seeing that he could manage to tie the knot himself,
but his hands folded over Fellyn's, and their fingers worked together to
tie the material into a firm knot.

"There...that should hold..." Fellyn said, still looking determinedly
at the knot rather than at Blake. Their hands were still entwined, both
reluctant to move them and both waiting for the other to do so. Luca's
throaty growl broke the tense moment, the dog remained curled
around the baby but her ears flickered up tall. Fellyn's hands dropped
and she hurried to scoop the infant to her arms. Ignoring the carrier,

she picked up her wineskin and handed it to Luca who took it in her powerful jaws and followed Fellyn as she ran full speed in the direction they had been travelling. Blake, turned to look to where they had come, to where Luca had growled, and seeing nothing but the trees he ran after Fellyn, not daring to call to her as he went.

Jared heard a familiar scream but he could not place it, he was shocked to a panic fuelled state of determination. He hastily doused the fire and covered it over, masked his footprints and hurried on into the thicker tree line, hoping that the cause of the scream was not coming his way. He did not want to be found out here hunting Fellyn like an animal. Jared had dreamed of his feet being washed by a man who glowed, he had heard the man speak in a foreign tongue but he understood only that when he was filthy and disgusting, this man had cleaned it as easily as wiping a tear from one eye. Jared was moving faster, walking at speed through trees, doubling back as needed and following the best bearing he could to find the mountain path. He had been drawn to it because of Fellyn's past, hoping that she would be headed that way as he could think of no other heading she might take. He chased his fears through the trees, not stopping to eat but only drink and splash his face with water as needed. He was moving instinctively away from that scream, hoping that the cause was not close by.

They moved through the trees like a herd of powerful animals, tearing down branches in their path and fuelled by the thrill of killing the old hag. Garrek walked out in front, Voit was on his left and close to his shoulder. They were pushing the men harder and harder, determined not to go home empty handed this time. They had found a camp and were driven further by its fresh covering and the warm embers it had hidden, whoever had been there did not want anyone to know where they were heading. They kicked the leaves and ransacked it for signs, finding only a half print near the river bank, so they crossed it, and followed its path uphill. Prey always ran with the water.

Jared had stopped running, he had realised how mad he seemed, going full speed in an unknown direction, following his gut rather than knowledge and running in circles from a completely unknown quantity. His pride kicked in and he set another camp, without a fire this time, erring on the side of caution for now. He ate an apple from a tree he had passed a while back, it was a late apple and was covered with holes. Jared picked out a small worm from the inside as he took a bite then carried on eating, famished from his day without any food until now. He leaned against the oak he had sat down under, and rested his head, intending only to catch his breath for five minutes.

Strong hands forced him up off of the ground, a hand closing his windpipe shut so that his whole body screamed out for air. He was losing his grip on reality and couldn't understand where he was. A face swam into his view, a brutish face with a scar across the nose, an ear crumpled and scarred too. Jared could think of nothing to do but scramble with his hands against those of his attacker, he tore into flesh and saw no hint of pain cross the face in front of him.

"I know who you are, Jared the hunter, fancy seein' you out 'ere too!" Garrek taunted. "It was me what burned down that dirty hut of yours an' now you're out 'ere and likely lookin' for the same thing we are!" Jared's eyes bulged hearing the confession from this man, his heart going as fast as a deer in the hunter's chase. He swung for Garrek's face, but the man moved and laughed at his feeble attempts.

"You can make this 'ard, or make it easy. We want the girl. We will pay you for 'er." Garrek said slowly. He bent closer to Jared's face, "pay with lettin' you keep your life." He said tauntingly. He shoved harder on Jared's throat for a second then released him. Jared slumped to the ground, his heart racing and his mind foggy while his air supply rectified itself.

"I don't know what you mean." Jared croaked, hoping to play dumb and escape somehow.

"Oh I think you do, an' I think you best play along hunter boy, else we'll kill that little baby of yours too!" Garrek said these last words slowly, and as if there were a need to convince Jared further, Garrek nodded at Voit, and the hulking brown-haired brute pulled something off of the back of his belt. Tehya's severed head, eyes rolling, mouth gaping, stared back at Jared. He retched and found himself desperate to hold on to the contents of his stomach but finding it impossible knowing what these men were willing to do and were going to do to his wife if he handed her over, or all of them including his darling daughter if he did not.

He dragged his eyes from Tehya's head and looked at his feet, he was dizzy and losing focus. *Think* he told himself. Jared thoughts raced, trying for an alternative option, killing these men was one option but he was outnumbered seven to one. Leading them to a trap was another, but he could think of no way to trap them and he had no help from anyone. He briefly considered tracking Fellyn with them, and rescuing his baby and allowing them to take Fellyn, she would do the same if it were about saving Etana, but he had come so far to save her from himself and now she had more desperate fears to run from. Jared thought of her running from their burning home, how she would have been so brave to get out with Etana and manage to run before these thugs followed. Jared realised that all this time he had been chasing her to apologise, he could do much more than that by saving her from whatever these men would do to her.

'I will find her for you, if you will promise to let me go with my child…safely." Jared said, defeated.

"We have ourselves a deal then!" Said Garrek and thrust out his hand palm facing up. Jared looked at the hand and the one who held it out, he went to place his own hand atop it in a gesture of agreement but Garrek grabbed his hand and twisted it around causing Jared to cry out. "If you try anythin'…heroic or stupid…I'll make you watch me as I rape that pretty little wife o' yours. And then I'll kill 'em both in front o' your eyes." Garrek grinned, and then shook the hand he held.

Voit came and tied Jared's hands together tightly so that his fingertips gained a blue tinge to them. Then he bound Jared's feet with only a small length of rope which would make it impossible to run. Finally, Voit tied a noose around Jared's throat and tugged mockingly "I would not run if I were you!" He said, and pulled harder to make the rope taut and strong on Jared's windpipe, clearly emphasising the point that escape was not an option.

They had been running or walking at great pace through the trees all afternoon, the fear back at their resting spot had dissipated and Fellyn had allowed Blake time to carry her precious cargo. He had loved holding Etana and chatted to her animatedly about the forest around them. When they had paused to drink and fill the wineskin, Fellyn had asked to take the baby back, needing to feed her quickly anyway. When they had moved out again, Fellyn had tied the baby to her own chest, feeling intensely needy of the uncomfortable weight as reassurance.

Blake and Fellyn had reached the edge of the mountains, the trees dotted sparsely in front of them scaled the steep incline and had a thicker quality than those around the castle had been. Fellyn breathed out an exclamation at the sight of the snow tipped mountains, she was

116

stunned by the beauty and felt like she was on her way out of all the problems that plagued her life. She snuggled up to Etana and turned so that the little baby could see the mountain view, Etana just wriggled in excitement and squeaked as Blake came into her line of sight. Blake smiled at them both, took Fellyn's arm and the pair walked along the line of trees, looking for the path through the valley that Blake knew was near them since he did not fancy climbing with an infant's delicate frame to worry about. Luca was bouncing ahead of them, nose shoved deeply into the long grass, on the scent of an animal and hungry for a meaty meal.

Fellyn stared all around her and took in a big gulp of mountain air, it was sweeter and clearer somehow. "Let's hunt first, Blake, I don't think we will find much in the valley, we ought to stock up on game and fruit." Fellyn said, thinking ahead to the long journey through the mountain pass.

"Good thinking! Luca's onto something, do you want to go or shall I?" He asked.

"I'll go, we make a better team." Fellyn winked at Blake, she was relaxing more the further they moved from their old camping site.

Fellyn handed her tiny bundle to Blake and he took her gladly, settling himself in the thick damp grass to cuddle Etana.

Fellyn sighed, her back straightened and she stretched her arms out high. Luca's face shot up out of the grass and her ears pricked excitedly. "Let's go Luca, where is it?" Fellyn asked of the dog, Luca's head returned to the grass, sniffed deeply for a second and then she began racing ahead, pausing here and there to let Fellyn catch up or to plunge her snout into the grass. They moved through the trees for a while, Fellyn had the knife they had gotten in the castle in her right hand and she strode gracefully, making as little noise as possible, they were quite a way from Blake when she heard voices near her. The light was fading so she huddled into a bush, Luca calmly at her feet, they hid for a while until she could see many men far in the distance, the last one of them stumbling roughly and slighter built than the others. She noticed the bindings around his feet and squinted, shifting her head slightly to get a better view, then she recognised the thin cloak she had sewn, and the boots she had darned many a time. It was Jared.

Chapter 12 – The Hunter

Jared was directing them to the furthest side West of the mountain range, where the land was covered with smaller hills and gorges, it was a good few days hike and was a lot wetter than the lands to the East. Rolling mists came in close there and he was hoping that if they got into that hilly and misty area, he could slip away from them easier and escape. It was a wild plan, but he had been thinking of setting off a rock slide onto these men, he fantasized about them being flattened by boulders while he stood on the hilltop above them and watched. Or perhaps watching them being eaten by a mountain lion...

The rope tightened around his throat and he moved a little faster, they had been periodically beating him to try and squash and confidence he had and also for enjoyment, Jared could see it in their eyes. He kept his mind wandering to happier thoughts, pushing them to the West of the mountains, determined that he would at least get a safe distance from Fellyn's tracks to give her a fighting chance, when they asked, Jared was jabbering about Fellyn being scared of the mountains so there being a likelihood of her aiming for the hills and gorges. They were happy with his answer, and he had seen two of the smaller men, named Korx and Ravvur, talking quietly about that, they had mentioned young girls Seraphia and Althia, names he hadn't recognised, and about ice but he was too far back held by Voit to hear them much more. Jared busied his mind with concentrating on his captors' weaknesses, Voit had a slight limp and Jared was trying to figure out why and where in the leg the injury could be.

Another man, whose name Jared had not heard, was quieter and often pushed around but he seemed to be the least brutal. This man had not touched Jared and did not look at him, Jared had seen him wince when Voit crossed his path with Tehya's head swinging from the belt. Jared saw this as an opportunity to play on the man's less thuggish nature than the others, if such an opportunity were to ever arise. These men did not suffer fools gladly, they were constant on their watch and reign on him, there was always a man tugging on the rope or else whipping him with the other end of it if he dawdled. Voit enjoyed being the one leading their prisoner, but often rotated with Korx for his chance to wander ahead and talk with Garrek or else go to the trees to relieve himself.

They never allowed Jared a chance to stop to do the same, he had asked and been punched and kicked repeatedly in the stomach for voicing a need, meaning that he had already been forced to relieve himself where he sat during their overnight stop. They had beaten him again for this and dunked him in the stream, holding his head down until he felt his lungs threaten to explode before they yanked him up and started again. This had gone on all night and day, they were nearing the end of the day following his capture, and Jared's spirit was not beaten despite the brutality, he kept his mind clear and focused on their weaknesses, and obsessed a little about how to kill them all. He licked his lip, it was split in several places after being beaten and dry from lacking water.

Fellyn had run back as fast as she could once the way was clear of the men keeping Jared captive. She had run with Luca hot on her heels, the hare scent forgotten in the desire to put distance between her and those men. She had fallen into Blake's arms, Etana sleeping in her carrying cloth and some entwined leafy branches Blake had woven together as a sort of nest. Fellyn had choked out what she had seen happening, the men from the castle, Jared being led and bound as a

120

prisoner, their direction in the forest, everything she could remember was spoken to Blake in a breathless panic. Etana was roused by her mother's voice and was unsettled from having too little sleep so Fellyn had stooped and collected her little girl, snuggling her close to her body and sitting herself cross legged on the grass to feed. The baby had gulped deeply as the hormones had flooded both bodies, a calmer emotion swept over the initial adrenaline rush and a plan had been argued over and formed.

Fellyn now sat, running her mind over every detail again and again, they had followed her and Luca's path through the forest and then attempted to find the men's tracks, trying to figure out how best to get to Jared. Blake was still determined to convince Fellyn to leave him to his own devices and get themselves safely through Valley Pass, although he was concerned that being pursued, they would be condemned to certain capture if they were ambushed in the high walled, thin valley. Blake had reminded Fellyn of the reason she had run but she would hear nothing, and truthfully, his pride stung that she was so keen to rescue this man who had hurt her repeatedly and chased her out so far. Blake felt Jared deserved all he got.

The pair sat now, side by side and rather closer than they would have had they built a fire but it was far too dangerous for fire now, especially as evening was drawing close. Blake had Etana on his knees while Fellyn pulled her fingers through Luca's fur, drawing out burrs and thorns from the poor girl's thick locks and piling them up into a hairy and thorny ball next to her.

"What about when we find them, Fellyn, you said there was more than five of them, and there had been more than that at the castle I'd bet. How do you even think we can get Jared out of there?" Blake shook his head, the whole concept of rescuing Jared utterly ridiculous to him.

"I don't know yet, I suppose we could wait until they sleep and then get him…" Fellyn broke off, hearing how dangerous it was even as she said it.

"And what about Etana? Will we take her into danger too?" Blake said, one finger being grasped by the tiny fists of the baby.

"No...Luca can watch over her somewhere while we go..." Fellyn said quietly.

"What if you can't return to her maiden, she would not last long with only Luca to care for her." Blake stated in a gentle whisper. His blue eyes were deep with worry for Fellyn's mad mission, she was determined on saving Jared but it was a fool's errand, he could see how likely it was that they would both be killed and everything they had achieved would be gone. He was not going to let Fellyn get herself and her daughter killed for a man who couldn't love her to begin with.

"Well..."

"No maiden, I really must protest now, this is absurd. There are only two of us and with Etana in that count, one of us will be out of action, and since I do not possess the ability to produce milk it means I will be the only one on this mission. A mad mission to save a man I do not know and who I resent for his treatment of you, who is bound and tied like an animal by several men of large build who will have been chasing us from the castle." Blake's voice was rising.

"Fellyn, this little baby here is the most precious thing in the world to me right now; she deserves a fighting chance at a life for once so snap out of it. Jared is not coming back now, please let me take you to my village and we will get you both settled into a more happy life." He pulled her hand away from Luca's fur and held it tight. "Please. I can be to you what he never was, Fellyn. I love Etana like my own and I can love you as mine too..." His eyes were glittering with promises and emotion, and Fellyn believed him, but she could not forget her husband so easily as that, and would never forgive herself if she did not try to help him and forgive him for their past. She could leave if he was still the same, but would Blake wait for her? Selfishly she wanted to keep Blake's promises alive and hopeful for her, she wanted him to be there if Jared hurt her again. She needed to feel like a hero would be waiting for her after she attempted to fix things with Jared, because she would feel less guilty if it failed that way than had she not tried at all.

"Blake…I…I cannot promise love to anyone but him because I married him. I cannot just leave him with those men, what kind of wife would I be to do that? Blake, if he is safe and unharmed, I can tell him what I want now is a new life and to find my real home. We can send him back to Tebel to care for his family." Fellyn was telling Blake only half of what she felt, but he smiled faintly and looked at their hands, entwined and connected, until he had said it aloud he had not realized just how much he cared for Fellyn, this strange woman he had known only a few days, he could not watch her walk away with Jared out of his life, but he would not let the man die. He could not allow that kind of remorse and pain to hang over her.

"Fine…but you aren't coming with us, you and Etana will stay a safe distance, you will have to wait for me and if I do not return after two days, you are to head back to the Valley Pass and once you are out of it, follow the western path all the way to Callenham. The path is steep and the village is up within the hills but you should find it. When you get there you need to find a woman there called Forey and tell her who you are. She is my mother and she will take you both into her family and keep you safe." Blake was frowning now, one hand still holding her hand, and the other being gripped tightly by Etana's firm grasp. "If I do not come back to you in that time or send Luca back to you, then know that if I live, I will fight my way to come back to you at my home." He looked up at her face, it was completely unreadable.

Fellyn smiled and teased him "Then you would have three women to find on your mission."

Blake was taken aback, and he realized he had not even thought of his love in a long time, his mind was full of Fellyn and her child.

"I...I suppose yes." Said Blake, no hint of humour in him now. "But you will do this, Fellyn, or I will not go to Jared for you, promise me you will leave after two days hiding?"

Fellyn stared into the blue of his handsome eyes, she nodded and took her hand from his and touched the delicate palm to his stubbly cheek, holding him as passionately as she dared.

Blake put his hand on top of hers and gently removed it, not wishing this embrace to go any further since he knew that he could not usurp another man's woman again. Not even this one. If she truly chose to leave Jared then he would be waiting for her, but he would not take her from him, his time in the Temple had seen to it that he would never be capable of causing adultery in a marriage again.

"Yes, okay Blake." Fellyn smiled encouragingly. "Thank you."

Blake handed Etana to her mother and stood, needing space from Fellyn before he shamed them both in the heat of the moment. Fellyn held Etana up letting the tiny little legs kick at her knees, Etana was slightly floppy and cooing as usual, she was gaining strength each day.

From where he stood a few yards away, Blake spoke out, "we will follow their tracks until we know we are close enough to ambush but not enough for them to know we are there. You and Etana will stay further back and hide as best as you can. I will take Luca and direct her to distract them, hopefully they will follow Luca away from camp leaving Jared exposed. If that happens I will take my chances and go, hoping that Luca is faster than they are." Blake was planning a dangerous task and at her request, Fellyn prayed hard for his strength and their safety.

"Luca is fast, Blake, she will be fine." Fellyn could not think of any way to tell him how she worried for his safety without telling him how she truly felt so she just busied herself with making their beds and readying things for the morning. They sat in silence in the darkness of the night and ate the last of the fruit they had foraged. Fellyn fed

Etana and they both fell asleep, their beds beside each other to keep heat in since they had no fire and the air was cooler up here.

In the darkness, Blake listened to Fellyn's breathing as she slept, wondering if after tomorrow she would be a step closer to her husband and so further from himself.

Morning rose spectacularly, the sun was watery and bright, the morning was a picture of peach and magenta streaked across clear blue sky. Not a cloud in sight and the most beautiful of bird song was all around them, the birds blissfully unaware of the journey this group were taking today.

Fellyn and Blake had gone about their usual morning routine of water, cleaning and feeding before hurriedly clearing the proof of their camp from any passer by. As they made their way through the forest, listening to the babbling of the stream beside them and the chirps of the birds around their heads, they were on the lookout for both predator and prey. They needed game to eat well again, they had been surviving on fruit for a few days and this far to the mountains it was becoming sparse, winter was drawing close and the forest was preparing for the cold to come. Leaves falling all around them, rich browns and oranges in a dance of the seasons paved their way, muffling their footsteps and hiding their tracks.

Fellyn suddenly stopped as Luca halted and raised her paw in a fierce stance. About one hundred feet away stood a jackrabbit, head raised and ears flicking, listening for danger. It was a well fed animal, a good size and age and the idea of rabbit made Fellyn's mouth twinge. She put her long finger to her lips in a sign to Blake and pointed to their quarry. He smiled widely and raised his hand at her, questioning if she was taking it or him. Fellyn pointed to Etana on her chest and then back at Blake, he grinned harder. Luca was intent on the rabbit, and when Blake tiptoed stealthily to the dog's side, she looked at him for his direction. He pointed his hand left and forward, so Luca, body as close to the ground as she could get, moved slowly and stealthily around the animal in a wide arc, when she was across and left from Blake she stopped and raised her body a fraction, her shoulders high beside her lowered head. Blake had crept slightly forward and Fellyn had moved back into the shadow of a large tree, watching them from afar. Blake raised his hand in a signal to come and Luca sprang into action, her body going at top speed towards the rabbit, it turned and curved left and right trying to lose the dog hot on its heels and as it neared Blake, he moved from his crouch and scared it back nearer to Luca, the dog sprang and caught the animal's hind leg and it kicked her hard in the nose. Blake had moved in quick and threw the knife deep into the animal's neck, it squealed for a second and then lay still. Both panting hard, Blake ruffled Luca's fur and stroked the line of blood on her nose, Luca's tongue was wildly drooling as she panted hard, licking at the wound every now and then. Blake carried the rabbit back to Fellyn and Luca stayed close to his body. Fellyn welcomed her dog back to her with a stroke and kind words, she used a few of the last green leaves and some water to rinse the deep cut and it seemed better already. They moved to the stream again and Luca lay in the water and lapped loudly, Fellyn and Blake laughing about the hunt and looking forward to the meal it would bring. Until they remembered their mission and then fell quiet, neither one wanting to remind the other of the coming task.

While near the river, Blake cautiously built a fire while Fellyn skinned and gutted the rabbit, they cooked it quickly over the fire and then doused the flames as quickly as possible, hoping to ensure they didn't give off too much smoke. They ate the legs between them, and then wrapped and carried the rest of the rabbit to eat later on. Fellyn had sat the skin on the hot logs to cook, and gave it to Luca to clean up, Luca happily wolfed down the entrails too so they left nothing behind them.

They moved onwards through the forest, following the trail of the group of men, judging the tracks to indicate that there were eight men in total. Fellyn felt completely lost, fearful for Jared, but sending Blake in to rescue him was troubling her too. She decided to only follow half of Blake's request, planning instead to follow him closer to the camp and try to see what would happen, telling herself that she would not get involved for Etana's sake, but she could not cope without knowing what would happen to both of the men she loved.

Chapter 13 – Her Master's Side

Jared was watching the men around him, Voit was dozing off next to him which was a good form of entertainment since he had been lonely for a while. The man dribbled and snored before he was actually asleep, and every time his head flopped forwards as he was dozing off, it would startle him and a torrent of violent words would stream angrily from his mouth, gradually becoming a slur as the whole cycle began again. This kept Jared amused for at least twenty minutes before it became irritating.

He had also figured out that the rope was just long enough for him to stand facing away from his resting place and relieve himself aiming at Voit's feet while they slept and the one on guard wasn't looking or was dozing. It passed the time at least. They had become a little more lenient about toilet stops since Jared had endured a gassy reaction to some bad fish they gave him, for a toilet stop he was taken like a dog into a grassy patch, but it was an improvement not to be sniffed at when he had been holding it for days. Jared found that despite his situation, he was internally very cheerful, enjoying the scenery and thinking of old hymns from when he was a boy, he was gradually working through the lyrics to all of the ones he remembered. He had also been praying more, silently of course, but it was causing something of a calm demeanour to take over his whole being, which was clearly frustrating to his captors who rather liked to see people suffer. He sometimes tried a conversation with Ravvur; he seemed less angry than the others and was happy to allow Jared to drink and relieve himself when needed, something which was making him by far the favourite one to have on the other end of his rope.

Garrek, however, was getting more brutal each time he spoke with Jared. This man's pride was a delicate feather, it was all too easy to insult him and have a lashing in response for it whether Jared intended it or not. It was clear enough that Garrek was frustrated that they had not come across Fellyn yet and it would not be long before his punishments were not so easy to simply shrug off.

Jared watched the men sleep, Voit was meant to be on watch but had finally stopped his outbursts of anger and was drifting into a deep slumber. Jared was relieved for the peace and quiet to think about how he would escape these men and kill them all, it was rather tempting to steal Voit's knife from his belt and just slit their throats where they slept, but it was unlikely he would get through many before others woke and had him killed anyway. Jared decided to at least get the knife and try it, if he went down with three or four then it was a job well done and less for Fellyn to contend with. He shuffled a small amount closer to Voit, pushing himself into a firmer position ready to spring once his feet and hands were free, he reached out his hand and gently, easily even, slipped the blade from the sheath and flipped it into his hand, waiting for a sign of movement which would require him to hide the knife.

Fellyn was following Blake from afar, he had told her to stay in a thick clump of bushes with their water and food, to rest with Etana and concentrate on feeding her up and keeping them both quiet. He warned her to only relieve herself occasionally, and to keep the baby strapped to her at all times in case she needed to run.

"Stay hidden...stay safe, Fellyn..." He had whispered to her after babbling worriedly at her where they stopped. Fellyn had not known what to say to him as she watched him go on a fool's errand to save her husband. She had pulled him into an embrace that emanated heat between them and desperation for survival, holding him as tightly to her as was possible with Etana between them, Blake had grasped her shoulders in his strong hands and kissed her forehead sweetly. Fellyn had closed her eyes and leaned into him, wishing for that moment to never end. She sat in the clump of bushes, remembering how much her heart had flown at this simple gesture, and how it had turned in knots of fear when she watched him run quietly into the trees without her, towards the men that hunted them.

As Jared turned the stolen blade to tackle the rope around his wrist, he saw a great shaggy dog run right to the edge of the camp, it was Luca, he would recognise her anywhere. The dog saw him and Jared saw what could have been mistaken for a smile on its muzzle. Luca was panting, but she barked twice and then when one man was roused she turned and ran, pausing here and there as if to wait to be chased.

"A wolf Garrek, it's a bloody wolf 'ere in the camp!" Korx shouted, frightened of the unknown quantity. Garrek was on his feet, he saw the dog through the trees and shouted to the men to follow it, to kill it for its fur and meat. Luca bounced away into the thick trees, faster than the men and not perturbed in the slightest. Jared had been so stunned he had forgotten that he was holding Voit's knife, who was now awake and confused. It was only Voit and the nameless man left in camp in the confusion, they did not seem to know what to do, and in the moment that Jared decided to stab Voit and hope for the best from mr. nameless, Voit saw the blade and jumped to his feet. He had barely time to react when another man, completely new, tall and blonde rushed into the camp with a blade like their own in his hand, he ran at mr. nameless and a fight began.

Jared thrust the knife he held into Voit's side, who was unarmed except for his hold on the noose. As he went down clutching his side, he gritted his teeth into a snarl and yanked on the noose, closing Jared's airways. Jared fumbled with the knife, trying to sever the rope at his feet, once it was frayed and slim he moved on to the one on his hands, desperate. Voit had found a new wind and was scrabbling one-handed to get the blade from Jared, who was losing breath fast. Jared threw his hands into Voit's face in an attempt to punch, it was not too damaging but enough to get a better hold on the knife so he resumed his attempt to sever the bondage, it was not easy and he had little time before the blond man came to him and plunged a knife into Voit's back sending him crashing to the ground with a gurgle of blood from his mouth. The other man was nowhere to be seen.

"He ran, the other one, we don't have time, Fellyn is here, I came to get you." He puffed, he slashed at the ropes, catching Jared's skin a fraction as he did so and relished the moment a little, he had just released Jared's neck when the other men came charging back into their camp, furious at the situation and the clear diversion they had followed. Jared hoped Luca had gotten away.

Bodies plunged all around and back to back, Jared and Blake stood each holding a knife and attacked when a man came forward, for a while it was a simple circling and intimidation tactical game. After a while of this, Garrek charged at Blake, a brutally huge man and a good fighter, he went for Blake with all the force of an elephant and Blake met him at an angle having side stepped for the most part. A fist fight ensued as the blades were small, each of them trying to find a chink in the other's defences with which to plunge the knife to. Jared was now head to head with both Korx and Ravvur. Another man was down, Jared did not look to see who but he felt the crunch of bone under his feet as he danced and dived away from the knife attacks. He ducked under a punch from Korx and then threw his fist into Ravvur's stomach, winding him. Jared sparred with them like this until he managed to plunge his knife deep into Ravvur's neck, blood splattered all over the men, Jared felt it hot against his face and in his mouth. He spat it out, and Korx backed away a little as he was taken aback by the spray of crimson. Blake was beside Jared again, he was wrestling with Garrek and being forced down gradually, his face purpling and his shoulder weeping blood. Jared, in a moment of thoughtless risk, threw his knife and it hit Garrek square in the side of his temple, killing him instantly but leaving Jared unprotected. In that moment, Korx had grabbed a now unarmed Jared and pulled him into a headlock, backing away from Blake who now had no partner to fight and was coming for him.

Fellyn was sitting in a bush watching the fight, she had ducked when a knife was thrown her way, and held her breath and tried not to shout to her men as they fought, they were doing amazingly and it was all happening so fast. She had not kept count, but there was at least one man unaccounted for and Fellyn was looking for him. Just as Blake stepped towards Korx, who was holding Jared in a headlock with a knife to his heart, a man stepped out with a knife in each hand to the side and behind where Blake was ready to spring. Fellyn gasped and retrieved the blade from the thick bark of the tree beside her head, she didn't have time to think but breathed in deep as she took aim. The dagger left her hand fast, aimed at the man holding Jared with his back to her. Time seemed to move as if slowed, held back by the terror rushing in Fellyn's ears. Fellyn finally exhaled as she watched her blade plunge into Jared's stomach. Korx had turned at her gasp and instead of finding its intended victim, the knife had penetrated Jared's body instead. Jared doubled over, his breathing shallow in panic. He straightened and swung his arms out to hit Korx, who had been distracted, catching the brute in the side of the cheek and sending him stumbling away as Jared slipped to the floor with a cry of pain.

Blake had become aware of the man behind him, he grabbed a second knife from a body beside his feet and threw it at the man, missing narrowly. Fellyn sprang from her hiding place, needing to even the numbers and she heard Luca's heavy paws, springing into the camp at her master's side, hackles raised and teeth snapping. Both men raised their hands, and in the confusion and fear, ran away, the small party of survivors watched them go, knowing that nobody had an ounce of fight left in them.

Fellyn sprinted to where Jared lay, bleeding profusely. She pulled his head into her lap and cradled him, touching her hand to the wound that was gaping open since Jared had thoughtlessly ripped the knife from his body.

"Get me something to stop the blood!" She barked at Blake, he ripped the shirt from a dead body and handed it to Fellyn, who shoved it hard against the wound. Etana dangled facing forwards, strapped to Fellyn's chest and cooed at the new face before her, one she did not recognise any more. Jared shakily lifted his hand and stroked Fellyn's cheek and then Etana's. In that moment, the sweet joy of their defeating the enemy was overwhelming so it seemed too incredibly perfect to him. But Fellyn could see the colour draining from Jared's face as he smiled serenely at his family.

"I…I came to…find and say…" Jared was struggling, his breathing was heavily laboured and his mind fogging with the effort to stay conscious, desperate to take in every last second of his wife's perfect face and her beautiful smile, and to look on the face of his daughter with pride and love.

"I am so sorry." He choked. "My love…you are more beautiful than…than when I married you…" He smiled, he wanted to show her how God had changed him, how he had been saved of his anger. He wanted to tell her how many days he had thought of nothing but saying again and again how sorry he was, and how he had wanted nothing more than to hear her forgive him and to return home, together. He wanted to know that he had not broken this lovely wife that he had been so blessed with, and that he had not wasted his life on empty anger but that she knew he had loved her all along.

"I forgave you long ago my love!" Fellyn sobbed, stroking the hair from his blood spattered face, she kissed his cheek, his head and his mouth, her eyes brimming with agony as his pain tore through her gut. "I love you." Fellyn whispered, barely managing to hold herself together. Jared smiled sweetly and took great effort to tell her one more message

"Fellyn, they killed...Tehya...you, the house...they took you, Althia, Seraphia...you." Jared was losing focus now, and as Fellyn struggled to understand his last words, she simply hushed him gently, and kissed his eyes closed as he slipped gently into Heaven's gates.

Fellyn sat there a while, simply overwhelmed by grief and confusion, Blake was uncomfortable with the scene before him, and had been stripping the bodies of weapons and food and then piling them up. Luca lay beside Fellyn, whimpering as she sobbed over her dead husband's lifeless body. She held his strong hands and traced the lines of his face, taking in every little detail of him before she would have to say goodbye.

Blake came to her and knelt by her side, "he is gone, Fellyn, we need to get out of here. Let him go." He gently prised her hands from Jared's and she looked at him, her face blotchy and stained from blood and tears. She took Jared's hands once more and placed them gracefully over his heart. She said a prayer for his soul, kissed him one last time on his pale lips and then turned away.

Blake gathered what they needed and took her shoulders firmly in his hands, he steered her away from the grizzly scene and back to the path from which they had come. Luca lay beside Jared until her masters were out of sight, she licked his wound and nudged his face, whimpering gently. The graceful dog rose to her feet, howled for a fallen family member, and ran back to her master's side.

Chapter 14 – After the Storm

Fellyn was staring at her hands again, Blake was ushering her away from the brutal scene behind them and moving back to the stream heading to the Valley Pass. They needed to wash the blood away and clean the filth of the day from their shocked bodies, but Blake needed distance from the horrors of the day and thought Fellyn probably did too. Blake badly needed to bathe his shoulder which was still bleeding and felt like it had been set alight now that his shirt was rubbing against it like sandpaper. He was moving with urgency as if they were still being pursued though he was certain the two men that survived were not following them now, they had headed eastwards as they ran rather than Blake's return to the Northwest path so he felt quite sure that they were alone again. Odd, it seemed, that nothing had changed from yesterday, except that everything was different. It was still the three of them and Luca following the path to Valley Pass, they were still going to his home, they were still both alive and for the most part, fine. To think how they had danced care-free in the clearing not a few days ago seemed frivolous now.

He felt the sting of his shoulder as he moved his body sideways to take the brunt of a low lying branch so that it was swept out of Fellyn's path, she was locked in her mind, unspeaking and unresponsive but he daren't try to push her right now. He glanced at her again but she was still fixed intently on her hands, Etana sleeping soundly at her chest in the carrying cloth as if she had not just watched her father die, and Luca as close to her hip as it was possible to be. He was at a total loss for what to say to her to help, he could not even wrap his own mind around what had happened out there, how she had unintentionally killed her own husband. Blake saw the glimmer of the sunlight against the water's cool surface, he sent Luca on into the water and unwrapped the sleeping baby from her mother gently and quietly, not wishing to break the sweet peace that the tiny girl was encircled in.

When Etana was unwrapped from her mother, the binding tangled around her little legs and sweeping the forest floor, he laid her under the shade of a large tree, snuggled in leaves between two protruding roots so that she was supported in a strong embrace of nature as she slept. He turned back to Fellyn, who was standing in exactly the same place, silent tears streaking her cheeks and her hands cupped in front of her as if trying to contain something, her memories perhaps, or her sanity.

Blake went to her and looked her over, she was drenched in the blood that had poured like wine from Jared's body in her lap. She needed to be clean or she would never be able to snap back to reality. He bent to his knees and removed his own boots, then gently lifted her feet one by one and removed her feet from their protection. They were dusty and blistered from the relentless journey but she had not once told him this, he noted. Blake stood and softly wrapped his hands around hers which were still cupped and he led her like a child to the water. He stepped blindly backwards into the stream and took her fragile waist in his hands as he lifted her down the steep bank so as to stop her slipping on the soft earth lapped by the water. When she was stood in the gentle current up to the top of her thighs, her sewn skirt skimming her toned legs, she looked up at Blake, confused as she realised where she was standing.

"We need to wash the blood away..." Blake gently spoke to her, frightened for any adverse reaction. She simply stared at him, the tears still silently washing her cheeks in salted stains and her mind still trapped in the enemy camp. Blake moved slowly closer, not sure whether to take charge and wash her or try and encourage her to do it herself but after she stood there a while, he took her hands and moved them to the water, she allowed her back to bend with no response at all so he rubbed them clean under the surface. She had blood in her hair and on her face too as well as on her clothes, so unthinkingly he pulled her thick long sleeved shirt over her head, she raised her arms automatically and he slipped it off easily. She stood before him as a broken shell of herself but beautiful and mesmerising.

Blake took the wineskin from his belt and filled it, then used the water it held to rinse her hair over and over again, her hair falling between his fingers and down her back. When satisfied that her hair was clean, he moved it to one shoulder and rinsed her face and neck gently, using his fingers to wipe the last traces of Jared from her body. He wrung her top through his hands and then laid it to dry on the grass. He pulled his own shirt off painfully, wincing at the fire ravaging his shoulder. He wrung his own shirt out too, laying it beside hers. He assumed the current would have washed her skirt and as he wondered what next to do, she simply stared, face down cast and eyes brimming still. Blake's heart was breaking for the agony of the beautiful girl before him, he walked to her and finally, unashamedly wrapped his arms protectively around her in a strong embrace, gritting his teeth at the agony coursing through him at every movement. She broke down and sobbed, her head falling to his chest and her arms raised to wrap across his naked back, she had come out of her trance to a full wave of emotion. Blake could do nothing but hold her tightly while she cried away her pain until the rawness had subsided a little and she was empty of tears.

When she had been quietly resting upon him for a while, he removed his arms from around her and took the wineskin from where he had placed it on the bank, filling it again and holding it to her pale lips. She drank deeply, refreshing the dehydration of crying for most of the day, and he replaced it to the grass. Blake bit down on the pain in his shoulder and bent lower, he pulled her legs up and held her back supportively, sweeping her into his arms and stepped from the cold water to the river bank. When he had set her back on her feet and straightened, biting down hard to stop himself from crying out in pain, he saw just how cold she was standing there vulnerable before him. Gently he removed her wet skirt leaving her in only her undergarment, and then wrapped her thick travelling cloak around her again to hide her nakedness. She pulled it around herself tightly, relishing the warm covering from the breeze which was cooling in the dwindling daylight, and settled at the roots of the tree where Etana still lay sleeping. Luca had been sniffing the grass around their resting place, but came and laid her warm body on Fellyn's lap like a comforting blanket.

Blake hung their clothes out to dry on a thin branch in the sunlight, hoping they would be dry by sundown since he could feel the colder evening setting in. He hoped he had done the right thing by washing them and not condemned them to a night of fierce chill. He pulled his cloak back around himself, with only that and his undergarment covering him, it would be a little inappropriate to say the least to sleep near Fellyn. He glanced her again; she was tenderly stroking Luca's fur, which was a big improvement on her prior to their washing. He was so afraid for her, seeing that she was so pained by the day and all that had happened, he did not want to watch her grieve for a man such as Jared. Blake also knew that he wanted nobody else to comfort her now but himself, desiring to be her rock and support here and now. He went to where he had laid their carried things, seeing the key, the hastily cooked jackrabbit from earlier and the handkerchief he thought was lost. Blake flicked his gaze back to it, he was sure he had lost the token of his love at the castle in the water, yet here it sat like it had never been gone at all. He rushed to it and picked it up, running it through his hands and touching the weave of the lace on the trim. The old handkerchief reminded him of his childhood, of the woman he had loved and he felt a stab of guilt as he looked at Fellyn now, a woman he was willing to give up his past for and a woman for whom he would risk his life in saving her husband. A woman who was now free.

Fellyn was feeding Etana now, the wriggly little bundle held to her uncovered breast while Fellyn stroked Etana's cheek. Blake saw how good it was that she was returning to a normal function, and went to sit with her, the jackrabbit in his hand to encourage her to eat something. She leaned Etana closer in the crook of her arm so to free her other hand, took it gratefully and ate some, less than usual but enough to keep Blake from needing to force her to eat. Etana was sitting against Luca's curled frame like a chair, giggling at her own toes, unaware of the pain encircling their little camp. When they had finished eating, Blake took Etana in his good hand and gave the rest of the meal to Luca who ate greedily. Fellyn saw Blake wince at raising the baby to his lap, so she sat up and pulled Blake's cloak away from his shoulder delicately, a frown creasing her pretty face. She remembered seeing an injury during the fight, Blake's shoulder was red and inflamed though not dirty any more thanks to the cool stream, she looked at his face questioningly, not daring herself to speak yet for the pain threatening to overwhelm her again.

"I was stabbed by Garrek's dagger, it went in as deep as the blade but it's only a small puncture, I'm fine, honestly." Blake said with a smile, but Fellyn shook her head, concerned and then stood daintily, she walked into the trees and he watched her weave through the lower bushes of the forestry, sniffing the plants and rubbing them through her hands. When she had collected a bundle of stones, weeds and herbs she came back to him, laid a couple of large rocks down and put the plants on to them, she then took up another rock and smashed down on them, grinding them into a paste. She used her fingers to rub differing quantities together and then moved back to Blake, her fingers laden with the green paste. Fellyn gently rubbed the salve into his wound, the fire eased quickly and he felt a cool relief after a few minutes.

"What was that, maiden?" He asked, feeling the agony die down.

"Yarrow, or Arrowroot." Croaked Fellyn, her voice raspy from crying so long. "It stems the bleeding. And Laurel leaf for the pain."

She had finished with the mixture but left some on a rock, setting it aside to save for later. She went and dipped her fingers in the water to rinse the paste away, then returned and with a small bundle of leaves and knelt in front of Blake again. Fellyn carefully took each leaf and held it to the thick puncture wound, decided which one to use and laid it on to his skin covering the wound completely. She then took his belt from his trousers hanging in the tree and slipped it over the leaf, tightening it enough to hold the leaf in place, Blake groaned a little at the pressure of the belt on his damaged skin but he smiled at Fellyn while she finished what she was doing.

"Stay still, please." She whispered as he had shifted to look at the injury, while the belt held the leaf in place, she took Etana's carrying cloth which was made of a very long and seamless fabric, and slit a thin cut on one side, and pulling it through her hands had a sliver of the material about half and inch wide and very long. She went back to Blake and quickly removed the belt, in its place she lay the end of the fabric and repeatedly wound it from his shoulder to under his arm pit and twice around his whole back for a firm hold until it was tightly gripping the leaf in place and offering a stable pressure which offered relief also. She sat back to check the bandage and was satisfied "how does it feel?" she asked quietly.

"Great...thank you." Blake answered, glad of the help and for the occupying task that had brought her back from the intense grief consuming her before. With her awareness, however, came an awkward situation in that both Fellyn and Blake were incredibly conscious of being scantily dressed before the other's eyes. It felt strange to Blake to be aware and bothered by this, thinking how easily he had stripped his clothing when she had been just the girl in the castle, but now, here in front of a woman he loved but could not have, he was very unsure of himself. Fellyn cleared her throat and went to check to see if the clothes had dried, she shook her head when she saw they were still damp so went to sit back with Etana and Blake, the baby was babbling sweetly at Luca from her place on Blake's lap. Luca licked the tiny toes that dangled in front of her snout and Etana's responding laugh bubbled over like an infectious stew. Fellyn smiled for the first time that day and saw Blake's expression lift too. *It will get easier with time.* She thought, remembering the words Tehya had spoken to her when one of her beloved pets had died as a child. It would not be so simple now, but time would numb the pain she felt.

Tehya! Fellyn thought. Remembering Jared's final words to her, how the men had killed Tehya, and that he had heard them talk of two girls and Jared had said the names Althia and Seraphia. Althia was her

140

sister...the sister she had lost when she had disappeared under ice...those men must be connected to that... Fellyn dug hard in her mind for the memory she had recovered when in the castle, the men had been dressed the same, in skins and hides with spears and daggers, all built broad and tall and knowing the name of her sister and Jared had said they spoke of her. Fellyn's mind worked over and over the fuzzy memory and what Jared had tried to tell her, it all seemed too connected, could it be the same men who had taken her and Althia as children? But who was Seraphia?

"Are you alright maiden?" Blake asked, placing his good hand on hers which sat in her lap.

"Blake...did you hear Jared before..." Fellyn's voice broke and she couldn't finish her sentence. She was looking at his hand covering hers, at his strong fingers and tender hand.

"Fellyn, I do not think it best to talk about it yet...I heard only his apologies I did not wish to eavesdrop..." Blake had taken his hand from hers and was looking instead at Etana on his lap.

"Blake...he said those men killed my Tehya..." Fellyn whispered, feeling tears choke her again. "He said...he said they spoke of my sister Althia...but they...how could they...?" Fellyn was stumbling through her mind for the connections, trying in her brokenness to fit the pieces together.

Blake had looked at her when she had spoken the name, he felt a fierce flow of emotions through his body at the mention of a girl he had known. "Did you say Althia?" He asked her, shocked and awestruck too by this.

"Yes...she was my sister but I hadn't remembered her until the castle..." Fellyn looked at Blake, he was staring into her face, his eyes taking in every tiny detail from her thick dark hair to her lips like roses and her eyes the same colour as a deer's pelt. He moved closer, jostling the baby on his knee, and hurriedly placed the little one back in Luca's warm cocoon of fur. Blake moved to Fellyn, shook his head unbelievingly and asked as calmly as he could. "What else, Fellyn, what else did he say of Althia?" His urgency shocked her, and she struggled to stutter what she could remember of those final moments.

"He said a name, he said they spoke of me...and a name I didn't know I think...Seraphia." Fellyn spoke quietly.

"What was the name?" Blake said, grasping her hands firmly in his and holding them to his chest. "Did you say Seraphia?"

"Yes... I" Blake stood, pulled Fellyn to standing and held her out at arms length. He looked her up and down as if he were seeing her for the very first time and laughed. Fellyn frowned, utterly bewildered. "Blake what...?" She asked.

"You...Seraphia...of course your hair, your eyes...we were raised together in our village! I watched you grow up from a baby and I..." Blake was smiling at her like she was the richest jewel in the land and Fellyn stood there, still so incredibly lost. "Althia..." Blake laughed, his whole face transformed from what it had been five minutes before. "I have been searching the land, Sephie...I have been looking for my love and my best friend...I have been looking for Althia for seventeen years!" He pulled out the recovered token, the handkerchief he had kept that had belonged to Althia when they had been children. He handed it to Fellyn, who turned it over in her hands, she stroked the embroidered edging in threadbare cloth and saw the delicately stitched name of her sister along one corner. She remembered the little handkerchief, and she remembered her sister all too well in that moment.

It was too much to bear, her emotions were a confused chaos of agony and desire, and now frustration. She couldn't place what was boiling her blood in anger of everything, until she recognised the jealousy in her heart, tumbling through her, full of the fear that this man wanted Althia rather than her after all that had happened. Fellyn stood, totally at a loss and walked numbly into the trees leaving the

142

little group of her loved ones clustered without her. Air, she needed to breathe, her lungs were tight and weak as she stumbled to a thick group of bushes. She fell to her knees and flopped forwards, her head resting on the spongy grass as her hands beat the grass. Her heart breaking and her mind all too full, she sobbed until she felt she was as broken and empty as the burned home she had run from.

Chapter 15 – Woman of Water

Fellyn was wide awake, staring up at the moon which shone through a gap in two trees whose leaves were almost all gone. The moon was not quite full, in that stage it reaches when it begins to wane and looks as though a chunk has been taken from its wholeness, like a piece of it will be forever missing and that missing piece takes more and more until there is no moon at all, an empty space where there once was something so prominent it pulled tides in the ocean and gave light in darkness. There was always a joy too, when the moon waxed once more and became whole again, as if it were possible for something to be cut down to nothing yet restored in the same way it was broken, and brought back to full beauty despite the pain of knowing it would happen again and again.

Fellyn envied the man beside her for his ease of sleeping, for the gentle breathing that let her know she was utterly alone in her thoughts and for his calm and hopeful attitude to their journey. Fellyn instead could not stop picturing the blade leaving her hand and plunging into Jared's stomach, and the way his eyes slipped out of focus and completely changed when he died. Cold. Empty. She kept seeing that moment replayed when she closed her eyes so she had stopped trying to sleep and was instead just laying looking into the night sky, thinking over everything she had endured yesterday. Their ambush on the camp, her blade, Blake's wound and Jared...telling her of Tehya and Althia and of herself.

144

She wanted to ask so many questions of Tehya and Jared, of what they had heard, of how Tehya had died, for her dream had been so excruciatingly awful that she wanted reassurance that it had in fact been quick and merciful rather than drawn out and repulsive. Fellyn needed to ask Tehya where she had been found as a child for she could not recall meeting Tehya, she needed to know how she had not drowned in the ice, and what had become of Althia. Fellyn thought of her sister and longed for her, she felt closer now knowing that her name was Seraphia, although it brought no memories to her of that life, it just fit with Althia like a matching set. She could picture the delicate frame of her sister's face and her auburn hair so different to her own dark locks, of the slit in her iris that she realised now was where Etana had inherited hers. Fellyn could see the rope burn and frozen fingers on her sister's tiny hands and wished it had all been different, wished she had not crossed the ice.

Blake shifted beside her, rolling over so he was facing her now and though it was slightly strange and uncomfortable to sleep so close to him, she dared not move in case she woke him or Etana who was snuggled in Fellyn's arms between the two of them. Fellyn looked into Blake's peaceful face, admired his strong jaw and kind, sleeping smile. She was so desperate to know their history, to remember him from childhood as he had spoken of it but she could barely believe it were true because she still had no recollection of the past he knew, if it weren't for the fact she had already known she was not Tehya's daughter but had once lived in the mountains, she would never be able to believe Blake at all. His blonde hair slid forwards so that it fell over his handsome face and Fellyn couldn't fight the urge to stroke it away again with her free hand, when her fingers made contact with his warm skin his eyes fluttered open for a second, his hand came to hers and he smiled as he held her hand against his cheek but he fell asleep again quickly, muttering her sister's name as he slipped into sleep again, a warm and full smile still on his perfect lips. Fellyn gently pulled her hand away and irritatingly, the hair fell back into his face. She let it lie there this time, not wanting to rouse him again so instead snuggled closer to him with Etana and felt Luca move closer too against her curved back. There she fell asleep, book ended between her most faithful companion and a friend and brother from another life.

Rhia patted the goat, Grissy, she had been getting a good milk supply from her for over two weeks and was beginning to worry about Tehya. She had said she expected to be gone a few days but still she had not returned, Rhia had taken Marcus to Tehya's hut on the outskirts of the village where the forest thickened but the lack of food and water out for the hens showed that Tehya had not been home recently. Rhia had brought the hens and their large supply of eggs back to her home and after trimming a wing on each hen to stop them fluttering over the pen and away, had settled the hens in the enclosure that Cassius had originally set up to keep Storm from wandering.

Rhia had then distributed the eggs to the needier families in the village, Tehya usually did this herself, she had always shared her produce; the vegetables she grew and the milk she got, she tended to wounds for people with the herbs in her garden too and Rhia could not remember a time that Tehya had not been there for her when she had needed help. Rhia decided to send a scouting party of village men to search for her, seeing as it had been so long, but she had not said where she was going nor how long for. Rhia stood with the pail of milk in her hand, she took it carefully back to the house and brought Grissy some stale flat bread slivers to eat in return for the thick milk supply.

"Cass, my love" Rhia said to her husband, who was in their kitchen stoking the fire over which a pot was full of water to boil. "I think we ought to worry about Tehya, she has been gone such a long time all alone out there." She was being delicate, she did not like to tell her husband what to do as he was a proud man.

"Mmm?" Cassius turned to look at her, not really listening the first time she had spoken.

"Tehya, she has been gone a long time, should we not look for her?" Rhia repeated herself.

"Tehya knows the woods, Rhia, she's an old hat at all that lark." Cassius said, dismissively.

"It has been half a month since she set out with no telling of when she was coming home...I think you ought to send the men to search for her, she is elderly." Rhia spoke gently again, knowing best how to sway her husband after their eight years together.

Cassius sighed, "fine, dear wife, if it would please you then I will have the men search today for her. Do you know which direction she was headed, to Cabaro perhaps?"

"No...She did not say but Jared had gone that day also, perhaps to search for Fellyn and Jared?" Rhia thought out loud, realising that she had missed Jared's company during the afternoons when he would usually visit them. She felt a little sinking in her chest and tried to ignore its presence.

"I'm sure she is not far, dear. No need to worry, eh?" Cassius smiled, assuming that her downcast emotion was about Tehya, he knocked her chin gently in an endearing manner. Taking his cloak and hat, he left the small house, packing his riding things ready for his long journey to Varose for he was to leave at first light.

Rhia looked over at the bed behind the curtain that she shared with her husband, and not for the first time, wished that it were Jared coming home to her instead.

Korx was walking ahead, limping a little from what he assumed was a cracked bone gained from the fight with their prisoner.

"Hurry up, Slint!" He yelled back to the quieter man following him. Slint quickened his pace, not really wanting to be any closer to the man up ahead than was really necessary seeing as he stank to high heaven. And he was a child killer, which didn't sit well with Slint, it was a just something that was too evil to be considered acceptable. Slint had done time for theft and for killing a soldier of the King of Xandia, he hadn't intended to but he had been running from the man he'd robbed and had ended up in a fist fight with the guy. The soldier was there at the wrong time and took the hilt of Slint's blade to the temple during the fight, it had killed him rather than just knock him out, bad luck really. Slint hated taking a life needlessly, he would rather run than kill which had made him a weak member of the Sraug, he had been an easy target in the beginning of his training, but he had gotten a reputation as a hard hitter, he was strong despite his slight build, and was a deadly shot with a spear. Korx, on the other hand, was as stupid as he was strong, about as deadly as a concussed bear because his reaction time was slow. Slint wasn't sure why this guy had killed the child, but the whole Sraug knew he had done it, they all knew each other's business since humiliation was all a part of the training.

Slint was only a few feet behind Korx now and was keen to trade places, to be upwind and in the lead since he had a better idea than Korx of the quickest way back. Instead he just stayed in his place, unwilling to fight a pecking order that was already established and had done well at keeping him practically invisible most of the time.

"If you walk any slower I'll be draggin' you there by your ears!" Korx bellowed behind him, glaring at his comrade.

"Let's find water Korx, our jars are empty." Slint stated, as simply as possible since he knew subtlety wasn't a good idea.

Korx just snorted along with a nod, so Slint ran ahead of him, standing for a moment to figure his bearings compared to where he last saw the river, it was currently somewhere to their left, but they would need to cross at some point to get back to the barracks. Slint sprinted up a the steep bank flanking their left side, finding that being

148

higher up gave him a vantage point to see his surroundings, he saw the glint of sunlight reflecting from the water and could see a tree that looked to have some kind of fruit near the river also which made it an ideal resting spot.

"Water is this way, and food too!" He called to Korx, who was still pacing onwards in the wrong direction. Korx stopped and huffed, he did not like being told what to do by a weakling. But he was hungry. His rumbling belly over-ruled his pride and as he walked past where Slint stood, he shoved hard into the weaker man's shoulder, proving a point.

They got to the water's edge and were drinking when they heard a noise as sweet as any bird song, but like it were being amplified and echoed around the forest. Assuming it to be some form of animal they were unfamiliar with, they continued eating of the fruit which was tart and dry until they felt satiated. From then onwards, following the river along the bank, they made good progress through the forest, stopping here and there to drink or rest a while but mostly moving at a regular pace.

After a long day of walking, having only eaten the fruit that morning since they had found no animals to hunt, the men were irritable and hungry. They reached a place where the river had formed a ring around a small piece of land, created by the meandering movements of the water eroding the soil, but Korx and Slint weren't aware of this and instead used it as a place to rest for the night. The men had walked a fair distance and had no polite company seeing as each resented the other and had no common ground other than their previous misdemeanours. Each found a tree to lean against for the evening and dozed off, confident that they were alone here and that they would be undisturbed. As the moon climbed the sky over a backdrop of sheer dark, a song arose from all around Slint, he woke easily, hoping he was still dreaming for he ought to be more frightened than he currently was if this were real.

He looked about him at the water as it glowed with a coruscant light, emitting a sound like song underwater, he looked over at Korx who still slept at the tree opposite him, and then back at the water. It was beautiful, a light full of meaning and wonder and he was so invited in by it that he found himself rising to his feet and stumbling ungracefully towards the river. He knelt at the edge of the bank and peered into its shallow waters but rather than seeing the shimmering light or the rocky bed, he saw his own face but totally changed. He was an older man with a scar on his forehead, he had ragged greying hair matted around his ears and iron cold eyes. The brutality in his own face was surprising, as he had always been a baby-faced young man who the larger males saw as a weaker member of the group.

Slint reached out to touch the water and found instead that he was touching a woman who rose from the water as dry as if she had risen from pure sunlight instead. She was as bright as the glittering water, and so beautiful he was sure he had never seen a woman like her. Those strange eyes were so large they filled her petite face with their green depth and her nose slim and perfectly symmetrical, her lips were a deep crimson and as plump and shapely as two small plums with delicate lines carved across their skin. She had an iridescent quality deep under her slightly blue skin and her fiery red hair was smooth and full, but despite having risen from the water at his touch, she was dry and perfect. Slint wanted to run from this perfect apparition, the feeling of her skin under his own was almost unbearable. He also found himself wanting to kiss and touch her with a blazing desire. She tilted her perfect head at him and smiled knowingly as if she had seen his thoughts. She giggled and the sound it brought bubbled up around them and echoed through the forest. Korx slept on, unaware of their visitor, and when Slint returned his gaze to the woman instead of his sleeping comrade, she put an extremely long finger to her lips and then held out her hand to him, an irresistible smile on her face that reached her eyes and made them dance in the water's bright light.

He raised his own hand and a shiver ran across his whole body, when their fingers met, he felt a jolt through his stomach and a pull he had no option of resisting for she was a magnet he was captivated by

150

and a presence he was incapable of denying. She drew him into the water and when he was completely immersed, was suddenly terrified of the creature before him for she no longer had red hair that blazed like fire, nor green eyes that danced, she was still beautiful but terrifying and her hair was jet black, spread out around her and swimming, lengthening through the water, surrounding his body and pulling him tightly like rope. He looked at the eyes that were full of hatred and laughter combined, and saw the girl he had chased to the river all those years before. A girl who had been trapped in the ice but with a slit in her iris that reminded him of who she was.

Slint woke with a start, had he dreamed it all? He could still hear the singsong voice of the glistening water and see the image of the girl in his mind. He shook his head, trying to displace the feeling that it had been real as he went to the water, peered over the side and saw nothing but the stars glinting off the water's face and the rippling of the flowing current. The dream had felt real...so incredibly real...and the guilt he felt about the girl in the ice choked at him, making him realise that he no longer wanted to return to the barracks and face the others who were part of that patrol group. He instead wanted to run far from here alone, to never have to see them all nor deal with them all but it was pointless to try, he would be hunted and found. Nobody just left the Sraug. Slint stood again, meaning to run from Korx's sleeping shadow, but he realised that he was damp. His feet, clothes and hair were wet as though he had indeed been in the river. Slint shivered, suddenly too frightened to be alone in the forest.

Fellyn was sat by their fire, her knees pulled tightly to her chest and her arms around them, staring into the flickering flames still unable to sleep fully. They had travelled back to the Valley Pass today, just tracking back the way they had come, but slower because Fellyn found she had little energy since she felt like the knife had been pulled from Jared's gut and thrust into her own. She was filled with guilt at his death, she had wanted to leave him yes, but to lose him forever...and at her own hand. She saw things too, probably through a lack of sleep, but things that she knew Blake could not see. She would shut her eyes and see her daughter, tiny and weak, swimming through water like a fish. Or she would see Tehya back at the hut working on a wounded animal, the images were obscure though, like her vision was out of focus and something was always off about them, the colours of the trees not the right green, or the face of the person she saw wasn't the right face but someone else's.

They were a jumble of painful thoughts and memories and terrified her into not sleeping at all. She was in a vicious cycle, desperate to sleep, but desperate to stay awake and she could barely keep her feet going forwards during the day. She hated feeling like this, so melancholy, so completely and utterly dejected. She realised that it was grating on Blake, that he was trying to be pleasant enough for the both of them but he was hurting too and she could see it. His arm was painful for him to use, and he was cut deep by her behaviour after their realisation of her past. Blake had assumed that finding Seraphia would be a magical reunion, that she would be glad as he was for the knowledge of her past. Blake was thrilled to find his old friend, he had talked of a girl he had loved like a sister while out building dens with her and Althia, he had said Sephie was like family to him and it was clearly a thrill to have found her in Fellyn. In all honesty, she would rather have been a stranger to him than hear that her own sister was his love. To know that this man had been searching high and low for her but had not thought to look for Sephie, who he apparently had loved like family. Like a sister. It pulled her heart and built a jealous fire inside her, totally engulfing her in emotion from Jared and Blake, she was red raw and could not find a way to heal.

While Fellyn's mind muddled through the confusion of the last two days, sat in front of the flickering flames and huddled alone, Blake was

152

laying with Etana in his strong arms. He watched her back shudder silently when she sobbed and saw the tension in her shoulders as she bore the weight of her world squarely on them. Blake did not blame her for Jared's death, and he knew Jared hadn't either, but she had taken it upon herself to be her own judge, to face her own trial alone and find herself guilty. She was shutting everyone out, even Etana.

Blake had needed to remind her to feed the baby several times during the last two days, he had handed her the squirming hungry infant and watched her clouded eyes wrinkle in confusion, so locked in her own pain she had forgotten the normal pain of hunger and a need for comfort, she was forgetting her child. It would not last, surely, it would come to an end when enough time had passed that the pain would dull. Blake had wanted her to look at him with new eyes when he saw her as Seraphia...as Sephie once more. She had only seen exactly what she always had, Blake being the man she met at the castle, and herself as a broken widow. Blake wanted to show her their childhood, the days spent climbing hills and making forts among trees and bushes, building their own pretend houses and talking of when they were all married off, all chasing birds and each other across the side of the mountain. It had all been a game, really, they were only eight or so...but he had cradled it in his own heart like a vow, like he and Althia had promised a life together but she hadn't held up her side, and here was Fellyn...Sephie, a sister he had respected and loved too, the mother of the group and destined for another man.

She had forgotten her friend in him, their adventures, their life. She didn't even know her mother nor the stories she had told them, the stories that they had heard as children, snuggled up in rugs by the fire holding a hot broth while Elenna told them about the prophesy as old as time, about the way rabbit had gotten his long ears and cotton tail, or how the dragons had hidden away with magic to protect their kind and the ancient ways. All the stories they had relished and re-lived out in their play houses, but here she was, the very same girl, and she was as far from him as she had ever been even when he had just found her. He thought of Althia more, of her auburn hair and unusual grey eyes, he had been absorbed in Fellyn but this familiar stranger had brought him a stronger hope of finding Althia. Blake was torn, he had searched for Althia all his grown life and still a part of him longed to find her. But he knew he loved Fellyn, he felt it deep in his soul and he wanted desperately to show her their old life together and help her remember. Help her to heal. He made a promise to himself to show her the girl she had been and the love she had grown up with and until she remembered that and made a choice…he would protect her as he had failed to do back then and would save her from what he couldn't before.

Chapter 16 – Changes

Fellyn and Blake were moving through Valley pass with the wind blowing through the tight corridor created by the sheer mountains with immense power, they were wrapped tightly in their cloaks but Fellyn had wished many times that she hadn't left the bluebell robe at the castle as she longed for more protection from the bitter cold. Blake had his arm around Fellyn's shoulder, pulling her and Etana tightly into his body to try and retain heat and at his suggestion, Etana was tucked inside her mother's shirt so that she was completely covered from head to toe. They had been moving through the pass for most of the day having reached it at late morning and Fellyn was bruised by the constant stream of memories that flashed through her mind. She kept seeing the ice, and Althia, seeing her sister's pretty hands red raw and frozen and seeing the men chase them from the cave. Other memories were tugging at her too now, memories possibly of Blake, for it was a boy of about her age and they were arguing over something petty, and chasing each other through the mountain village. She saw huts on stilts so that they were level on the rocky land, she saw goats wandering the town and she could remember the smell of freshly falling snow.

"We need shelter, Blake!" Fellyn called loudly to him, he nodded beside her, the wind loud in their ears and their faces tight from the cold, so much so that conversation was difficult.

They trudged on, closer to the mountain on their left side to search for crevices and caverns but there was nothing around them but the straight path in the freezing wind. Blake had said this path was a long and barren one, they would need to move fast enough so that their food supply did not have time to run out nor their water run dry, they were already parched and their mouths felt like they had been rubbed with a dry cloth for the wind had robbed them of any moisture. Blake picked at a brass button sewn into his cloak until it came off, he slowed Fellyn down and turned her to face him and took her jaw in his free hand, using a frozen finger he tugged her lip down to open her mouth and placed the button on her tongue and then pushed her jaw to close again. Fellyn frowned at him, not resisting him at all but confused, until she realised that having the button in her mouth had gotten her saliva flowing and her mouth returned almost to normal rather than paper dry. She smiled at him and they carried on walking into the harsh wind. Dark was creeping in but there was no sign of cover, it had been so long since Blake was last here that he had no idea whether he had in fact sheltered at all or if he had simply soldiered on.

A figure moved towards them slowly, alone and seemingly slight in build, Blake was on his guard and worried for the girls he shielded. Fellyn looked up at Blake's face, his jaw set tight and brows close in concentration like an animal ready to fight, she felt safe with his arm curled protectively around her shoulders and really did not want to have to move. They quickened their pace when Blake picked up speed, wanting to move past the stranger soon so as not to allow their faces to be seen for long enough to perhaps recognise them. When the figure was about a hundred yards away it slipped into a nook in the mountain that had not been visible from their distance and Blake stared after it longingly, weighing up the risk against the benefit of letting the girls shelter and rest. Deciding to follow the figure and fight it if necessary, he led Fellyn to the opening. It was slim and they needed to separate in order to squeeze through, so Blake went first and held Fellyn's hand as he led her in after him. A small cavern opened up in front of them and Blake walked over to where an older man sat on a rock which was one of many circling a fire pit dug into the ground.

"Well, hello there!" The man said cheerfully, smiling up at them and waving them to sit with him. Blake looked at Fellyn and she shrugged her shoulders a touch, undecided on the level of threat.

"Mind if we join you, sir?" Blake asked with one of his charming smiles.

"Not at all, in fact I'd be glad of your company young ones!" He said with a chuckle. "It's been a while since I've seen others around this path, where's your heading?"

Fellyn walked past Blake and sat on a rock fairly far from the man and sighed with relief at resting her tired legs and back, she pulled her shirt low to let Etana's little head poke free and the baby's eyes blinked furiously at the daylight in the cavern.

"Oho! What a lovely little surprise there!" The man's whole face lit up to see the baby and he clapped his hands together as he said "how precious, fancy having a wee baby this far out into the wilderness!"

Fellyn smiled, he seemed no threat at all so she lifted Etana out awkwardly from the carrier inside her shirt, the little feet catching on each piece of wound fabric as she did so. She turned the wriggling bundle on her lap so she was facing the stranger and Etana's eyes widened as she took in the room, her neck craning to look at the rocky ceiling above them.

"We're headed up to Callenham, well...we will be in morning." Blake said with a small smile.

"Oh yes, Callenham, lovely! I'm Sid, Sidney Bullrush!" He said proudly, holding out a hand to Blake.

"I'm Blake, this is Fellyn and her daughter, Etana." Blake shook Sid's hand and sat close to Fellyn.

"Well now! Blake of dark and of light, interesting...I wonder which you favour!" Sid leaned nearer to Blake, making the pair uncomfortable. "Fellyn...you are a passionate and control-seeking person, you favour tradition and rules...but there is something in you that isn't quite right about this...."

"Her name used to be Seraphia..." Blake said quietly and Fellyn looked at him, surprised and a little irritated at his suggestion that she was not who she had always been.

"Well then...Seraphia means close to God, fiery and passionate are very much still true, you delight in nature and have a love of beauty..." Fellyn looked at him, a personality analysis based only on name, it was ridiculous.

Blake laughed "that sounds about right!" He turned and smiled at Fellyn, but seeing her haughty expression, turned back to Sid.

"And Etana....well well...Strength of purpose she will have always, she is a thoughtful person and will grow to be a leader of others." Sidney slid from the rock onto his knees and moved closer to Fellyn and her baby. "But her eyes...the perfect keyhole to the soul...my dear she will have knowledge no other can ever gain!"

Fellyn just stared at him, confused about the relevance of her daughter's eyes, but Etana looked at the man and gently reached her hand to touch his crooked nose and babbled at him sweetly. Sid laughed and moved back to his rock.

"Now then, Blake. What say you and I build a fire for tonight?" Sid asked brightly.

"Well...yes of course." Blake answered, not daring to ask where he would find branches to build them a fire.

"Follow me boy! My dear, you will be very safe here please do not worry!" Sid said, patting Fellyn's head, causing her to glare at him for

158

the insinuation that she would be out of sorts without a man at her side. Fellyn huffed and nodded at Blake's questioning gaze, wanting him to know that she would manage just fine without him. Having another person had made her feelings shift towards Blake again, as if she had needed the realisation that she did need and want him. They headed back out into the howling wind and dying light, Luca followed them to the cavern's entrance and sat staring outside as if standing guard for her family.

Fellyn fed Etana in the calm and quiet, relishing the time alone since she had been with Blake practically non stop since meeting him. She stared into her little girl's eyes, the keyhole to her soul indeed, Fellyn could see what Sidney had meant, the hole in her iris did look rather like a lock.

"You are so like my sister, darling girl." Fellyn spoke to Etana, remembering Althia's eyes. "What can you see little one that I cannot?" Etana grinned broadly at her mother, a dribble of milk on her chin and her eyes glowing with wonder. Fellyn wanted to see her daughter grow into a wonderful woman, but to see her be a leader seemed a strange idea since she was not from a leading family nor born as a man. Perhaps influential rather than a leader, Fellyn considered their future and where they were going, the village, her village. Fellyn wanted to stay close to Blake, he was her rock now, her only link to this life, yet she did not feel comfortable any more in how she felt about him. Where before she would have enjoyed feeling his arm around her and his hand firmly on hers, she instead thought it was inappropriate and forced, strange the difference an old name had made...Fellyn thought that it might have been better to not have learned her past after all.

Rhia had helped Obe to organise the men into two different search parties, one group headed nearer Cabaro and one to the North in the direction Jared was seen going. Rhia had been helping the wives of these men today in thanks for their help and she had hot broth waiting for them all in her large pot, dusk was drawing close and she expected them all back before dark so she was sat with a few of the women from the village with mugs, spoons and bread ready for each of the nine men when they returned. Conversation flowed easily between the chattering wives, talk of the house being rebuilt for the missing Kellacks, the men finding the lost villagers and some silly gossip from Cabaro about an uprising in Varose.

Rhia hardly took any notice, thinking instead of Tehya, Jared and Fellyn and finding her heart yet again completely torn by how she felt about the whole situation. Iris was laughing loudly a few feet from Rhia and it all seemed absurd to her, here they were, waiting to hear whether a search party had found the three missing members of their village...and a baby. The women did not seemed bothered at all, in fact, they were behaving like this was a party when clearly it was becoming more likely to be a farewell. Rhia stood and rearranged the mismatched mugs for the men, she stirred the broth and sniffed it, it smelled very good and it ought to, Rhia had been making it all day, stewing the vegetables she could manage to get for it with a few pigeons she had been hanging since Jared last hunted for them. The birds had been hanging so long that they stank when she had plucked the breast and legs to pull back the skin and remove the meat, but the dark meat was well seasoned for it and would add a lot more flavour to the broth this way.

Sylvie came over to where Rhia was absently stirring the broth and placed her hand on the younger woman's shoulder. "I'm sure they're alright darlin'!" Rhia turned and smiled at Sylvie, it was kind of her to come and see that she was fine, but it seemed silly for her to comfort Rhia when she knew no more than anyone the fate of their friends since the fire.

The sound of hooves caught the attention of all the women and several stood to see the horse come into the village where they sat with the tables all pushed together in an odd formation among the flowers in the village square. A man none of them recognised came riding up

160

to them, and pulled his horse to a stop, jumping from the saddle before it had even stopped, stamping its hooves and tossing its fine head.

"I am looking for a Mrs Rhia Barrett." The man announced, one arm behind his back and the other held over his heart with his back straight and his head held high. He was a messenger, Rhia's heart stopped and she began to panic for her husband, why else would this man come here wearing Varose livery.

"I am she." Rhia said, stepping out from behind the table and walking with feigned confidence to the man before her. "What is your message?"

"I am to give the message in private, my lady, can we go inside your home?" The man asked, lowering his head to speak to her plainly.

"Yes...come with me. Iris, please arrange the food if I am not returned before the men are home and Sylvie...would you mind coming with me?" Rhia asked, aware that being alone with a strange man was both risky and likely to cause gossip, she wanted a witness to their conversation, even from behind the door.

Sylvie rose again and followed Rhia and the messenger to her house not too far away, Marcus and Davey were playing in the front garden with their wooden horses so Sylvie sat near them on a barrel and watched them while Rhia showed the man inside to hear what he had to say.

"Mrs Barrett, I have word from your husband." The man said.

"Is he well?" Rhia asked, feeling herself grow worried.

"He is fine, he cannot return home yet for a situation has arisen of dire importance, it is being kept secret until a public announcement confirms their decision."

"Sir, what has happened?"

"High Councillor Darue has been murdered." The man said in barely a whisper, Rhia gasped, and the man hung his head out of respect. "They are speaking of treason from the members of the council who seek power. Only a few of the counsellors are free of the interrogation and your husband is one of them, he is a favourite to lead when the council vote on a new High Councillor. He cannot return until we know one way or the other but he has asked me to tell you that you are to return the animals to Tehya, pack up what you need and bring the boys with you to Varose. He will be campaigning for the title in the next week coming and desires you be there to assist." The messenger finished speaking and waited, seeing the shock cover Rhia's pretty face.

"I need not remind you how important it is that this stay private, it could be a simple act of a power-hungry Councillor, but it may also be assassination as a threat of war."

"War…but against whom?" Rhia asked, confused by the overwhelming information.

"I cannot say my lady, but it would be devastating if our enemies found out our planning." The man nodded gravely at her and tipped his hat. "My lady I rode for many days without good rest, your husband promised bed and food before I lead you safely along the path to Varose tomorrow."

"Of course, we have food out in the square please join us, and we have room for you to stay." Rhia had so many questions, her brain fogging with what to do since Tehya was not home to have her animals returned and she had no idea how to pack to ride to Varose when she had no horse.

"How will we travel there when I have no horse for myself nor for my boys?" Rhia asked.

"We are to go to Cabaro first, we are to buy two new and well bred mares for your husband's stable in Varose and we will ride with a lad each, the third horse will carry your belongings my lady." The man stood proudly again, clearly pleased that he had been chosen to carry out an important task such as this.

Rhia nodded and led him through the village to the square once more, Sylvie with Marcus and Davey followed them as they went. The square was bustling with the returned search parties, men carrying steaming mugs of the broth and hulks of bread stood comparing their search, Rhia scanned the faces as she neared the group and realised that Tehya, Jared and Fellyn were not among them.

As she approached the table, Obadiah came to her and sadly shook his head. "No sign of any of them in any direction."

Rhia just nodded and touched his arm kindly, she had no words to say now, and she would be leaving first thing tomorrow. She turned to Sylvie and said quietly "how much did you hear?"

"Nothing, love, I did not listen." Sylvie said wholeheartedly, and Rhia believed her.

"Well I am to leave at first light with my boys for a long visit to Varose with Cassius, I have been keeping Tehya's hens and goat safe but cannot take them, will you keep them safe...until she returns? I will be home in no time." Rhia said bluntly, wanting Sylvie to think it was a routine visit and not a complete shake up of their lives, needing the woman to be unaware that if Cassius got the position as High Councillor, they would probably not return to Tebel again.

"Of course, sweetheart." Sylvie patted Rhia's arm and led the messenger to the broth and bread so that Rhia could sort out food for her boys before she returned home to pack for their journey.

163

Blake and Sid retuned from outside with their arms laden with dry logs and twigs, laughing and joking merrily. Fellyn scowled at Blake, she was not sure why in particular, but she was unhappy about his easy conversation with the strange man. Sid set to work building a fire in the sunken pit and Blake went back outside to bring in more wood, Etana was curled up in Fellyn's arms sleeping soundly while the men worked on warming the little cavern.

Once a fire had been lit and was casting dancing shadows on the cavern walls, Fellyn relaxed a little, feeling silly for having been so irritated by Sid telling her what her names meant. She thought about Althia, and decided to ask Sid what that meant too.

"Sid, if you don't mind me asking...would you tell me the meaning of another name?" Fellyn asked him softly.

"Of course, my dear one, ask away!" Sid said happily.

"Althia...she was my sister." Fellyn said in barely more than a whisper, Blake shifted in his seat and raised his head to Fellyn, and then to Sid to hear the man's answer.

Sid thought for a minute and then answered. "Althia is wholesome...a healing herb and a deeply passionate woman." Fellyn smiled at his answer, remembering her loving sister who had relied upon her so much. "But...Althia is a bitter woman also, she holds on to trespasses against her and she retaliates with a cruel heart." Fellyn stared at Sid, unsure about the last piece of wisdom since her sister had been a gentle character and Blake, too had not one bad word to say of her. Fellyn looked over at where Blake sat, with his hands clasped and his eyes staring into them as if they held the most fascinating of sights. Perhaps he did recall that part of his love. Feeling a stab of emotion at seeing his reaction to their conversation about Althia, Fellyn decided to change the subject.

164

"Blake, you said we used to listen to the old folk tales as children, didn't you?" She smiled at him, wishing he would focus on her as he did Althia.

"Yes. Your mother would tell us tales while we drank the green tea she brewed before bed." He smiled wistfully, remembering the warmth of their childhood.

"Sid, do you know the old tales? I would love to hear them but have forgotten since I was a child." Fellyn asked sweetly.

"Oh yes! I know the tales...which one would you like to hear?" The man chuckled and reached down to a brown saddle bag at his feet, he pulled out some little round cakes and handed one each to Fellyn and Blake. "Is the little one eating yet?" He asked.

Fellyn smiled. "No, not yet, though it won't be long!"

"Well eat young ones, they're a bit tough after a few days on the road but they taste good!" Sid bit into his cake as he held his free hand underneath to catch crumbs, wasting as little as possible. Fellyn bit the cake, thinking that Sid was right about them being tough, but it tasted of honey and elderflower and was delicious as if newly baked. Blake was enjoying his cake too and finished it quickly, Fellyn looked at Luca who was lying over her feet and staring at her master. Fellyn broke off some of the cake and gave it to the dog, thankful for her company as always. She would hunt for her as soon as she saw a chance, the dog needed a good meat meal, she was thinning around the middle and her face was leaner than it had been.

Blake patted his hands on his knees and said "how about the story of the prophesy?" Sid smiled at Blake and put the last bite of his cake into his mouth.

"The prophesy...well then..." Fellyn slid off the rock onto the floor and leaned against it, settling into a comfortable position. Blake got up and sat beside her, she looked at him curiously as he put his arm around her shoulder and pulled her close, she drew her knees up with Etana still laying on them with her arms stretched out to the side, her eyes opened at the movement and her confused face took in her surroundings and her mother above her, comforted, she fell back into a peaceful slumber.

"They say the prophesy comes from the land of mist and marsh to the east of Xandia, they say that the folk living there bathed in springs which were hot and blessed, these folk used many ways of talking to those closer to the heavens and so had knowledge others desired. Folk say that they could foretell a death of a villager. Some say that they know when storms will wash away their homes so they can move them to safety. The stories say they grew confident in their wisdom, they grew lazy with their prayer and they stopped asking for knowledge, and so a storm came through their village and destroyed everything in its path, homes and livestock were washed away and their crops failed for years after. The lands were diseased and their children starving. They turned back to their springs and found that they had cooled, their power dimmed and in their laziness, the generation had not learned how to ask for wisdom like their parents and grandparents had before. One child came who had eyes looking into heaven, eyes milky white but for the blood red lines that came when he would see what their Lord could see. He told this prophesy and we await its fruition:

When the fair of face become a king,

So a new world will be ushered in,

Brother agin brother and kin before kin,

To undo an age old sin,

A fair one born with a simple tell,

To see through eyes looking into Hell,

166

Before the time to be restored,

The child will break the dissonant chord,

Then be drawn blood from own blood,

Will cleanse the land by filth and flood,

In time will bring a peace unknown,

A reunited kingdom's thrones,

And once again man shall stand,

To rule before united land.

Some tell that this speaks of a war with Barabel, some say it cannot happen now that we have our counsellors not a king, but all are agreed that to disrupt our peace will cause our country to be shaken and damaged and will be bad for us all..." Sidney finished talking and the cavern was a hushed buzz of anticipation.

"Thank you, Sid." Blake said with a curt nod.

"Not at all, young Blake. We ought to sleep, let your lovely lady rest that pretty head!" Sid smiled at her and Fellyn blushed, wanting to correct Sid, but wanting to hear Blake's correction even more. Blake simply smiled back and pulled his arm from around Fellyn's shoulder.

"Sleep sounds perfect." He said in Fellyn's ear and his warm breath sent a shiver over her causing her heart to flutter wildly in her chest. He bent to Etana and kissed her forehead, she was sleeping once more and Fellyn carefully put her hands under the little girl's arms and pulled her tightly to her chest. Blake looked around and realised that without their usual bed of leaves, they were in for a cold and hard night sleep. Thinking quickly, he bent to Fellyn and untied the cloak from around her pale neck and slipped it from around her shoulder. He rolled it into a thick lump and placed in on the floor beside Fellyn, she looked and him and he helped her ease herself down slowly so as not to wake Etana. He swiftly removed his own cloak and lay down with his back to the rocks, curling himself around Fellyn and the peaceful baby in her arms, he covered them with his large cloak and in the slight awkwardness, put his arm around her. Fellyn shifted her body into the curve of Blake's, thinking how comfortable it was to be held.

"Goodnight, Sid." Blake said in a hushed tone.

"Sleep well young ones." Sid said from his own little makeshift bed, Luca moved closer to Fellyn and lay herself like a barrier between Etana and the world.

"Goodnight...Seraphia" Blake whispered into Fellyn's ear and leaned forward just a touch to kiss her flushed cheek. Fellyn had no response so instead moved her hand to Blake's, feeling his warm and rough skin under hers, she fell asleep curled in his protective arms, the firelight casting dancing shadows on the cavern's ceiling.

Chapter 17 – Journey's End

Rhia was travelling the well worn path between Cabaro and the northern city of Varose high in the mountains. She was riding a stunning black mare with a perfect swirl of white on her forehead and a beautiful long mane, this horse had character which was why Rhia had chosen her. When they had been inspecting the horses for sale at the market, Rhia had seen many which would have been solid to ride and good brood mares for when the time came, but she had seen this particular horse's eyes follow her around her immediate area, tossing her head proudly and practically dancing on the spot. Rhia had watched as the messenger, who had now introduced himself as Rowan, had lifted her hooves and tail and checked her teeth, the mare had stood beautifully and allowed him to inspect her with a sort of excitement that Rhia took for a good work ethic, so she had won on that principle and been named Jezebel for her beauty and alluring personality. Rhia had little Davey sat in front of her, they sat comfortably astride the four horn saddle and followed Rowan who had Marcus riding with him, Marcus charged with holding the reins for the second mare they had purchased, a smaller chestnut mare who had already been named Bracken and had a calm and gentle personality while being young enough to have many years of riding ahead of her.

The group had been travelling since midday when they had finished purchasing the horses and their saddles from the market and had eaten their fill of the venison stew served in the tavern. It was a cool day with a bitter wind biting at their fingers on the reins and blowing leaves up all around them as they pushed onwards. Davey had been singing the old river song to his mother as they rode and Rhia smiled, she loved to hear her boy sing since he had the voice of an angel.

"...Where willows touch the water's skin,

A lovely lady sleeps within,

She waits for passing men who toil,

And at their slumber doth uncoil,

And sleep they do though folly it is,

To run and hide from lady's kiss.

Sing ayeee oh, ayeee oh,

Sing oh the wandering men, be bold.

Sing ayeee oh, ayeee oh,

For some will heed the warning told."

"Stop that singing, Davey, it gives me the shivers!" Marcus called back from where he rode in front of Rowan. "And anyway, that song is for girls!"

"It's not!" Davey shouted back, his young feelings bruised by his big brother.

"Marcus you leave him be, he knows I love that song, don't you Davey my boy?" Rhia kissed his head and squeezed him a little harder, he giggled at her playfulness.

"Mother, is that story true? Is there a lady in the water?" Davey's voice was low, barely a whisper above the steady clopping of their horse's hooves.

"No darling one, it's a tale passed for many years, but it is only a story!" Rhia smiled at his innocence, he was only five years of age and her tender baby still, but he was leaving her lap and would be a lad soon, she sighed at this thought for she hated to think of him growing up and losing need of her.

"Mother..." Davey whispered again.

"Yes my little one?" Rhia asked gently in return.

"I wish it were true, I want to meet the water lady!" Davey giggled quietly.

Rhia grinned from behind him. "Well my son, just because nobody has seen her doesn't mean she never was seen! If you find the lady of the river, will you tell me?"

"Yes mother, I'll tell you, and then I'll marry her!" Davey laughed out loud and kicked his legs in excitement, causing Jezebel to dance a little in her stride and Rhia to tug on the reins and hush the horse, laughing and smiling with her son because his sweet innocence was contagious and precious.

Korx and Slint were making steady progress towards the borders of Xandia, following the line of the mountains on their left and trying to ensure they walked until they found another stream from the mountains before settling for the night, it had been almost a week since their camp had been invaded and they were still progressing towards the barracks. They had to get out of Xandia late in the evening so as not to be seen, if they were caught trespassing over the border they would be fired at, but the borders were only patrolled near the watchtowers so it was likely they could slip through on the cover of closing sun when the men would likely be swapping shifts. As they had progressed through the area, Korx had relented into allowing Slint to take control of their movements, he knew the area better and was good with directions, and at finding them food and shelter. Korx felt out of place in these woods, he was familiar with the mountains to the North and the land far beyond that, but it had been Slint who had once lived in the South, in the fishing villages on the coast so he knew these lower lands. Slint had felt uncomfortable in the shift of their positions, but it was an unspoken understanding, and Korx showed no sign of bitterness because of it so he simply took up the post and tried to lead Korx without insulting him. They were living from late fruits and berries as well as a few smaller fish that Slint had managed to catch using his spear and cloak, both men were starving and couldn't wait to return to the barracks to see a good meal, no one could argue that they were well fed there. Slint had wondered several times if they were fed well to bulk up weight and power, along with their fierce training, they were forged into a force to be reckoned with and most likely a deadly army.

Slint was still affected by the dream he had of the woman in the water, she had been so like the girl they chased that it had frightened him greatly and meant that he had been careful going into the water alone, he tried to bathe near Korx so that if anything happened again, he at least had someone to cover his back, not that he thought Korx would help him but it was a comfort to be with someone else where his nerves failed.

He thought often of their journey and a way to escape the impending wrath that was bound to come when they returned to the barracks without the girl, again. This time they would be returning as only two of the seven and he dreaded the torment that came when defeat had to be acknowledged, especially since they had been defeated by the girl and her companions...and a dog. Slint shivered in the cool breeze, wishing he had dared to leave Korx when he had considered it that night with the water woman, he could not shake the feeling that she was watching, waiting for him.

About a mile or so from the border to Barabel, Korx and Slint rested and washed in a noisy little brook running down from the mountains, they decided not to catch food to eat since they hoped to be back at the barracks by the following noon and were too eager to have a decent meal rather than waste time on catching a measly portion of fish. They sat to decide on a plan to cross the guarded border, since it had taken a rather elaborate diversion tactic to get all seven of the men through when they had set out several weeks ago to find the girl that, rumour had it, was alive and well living in one of the forest villages. This time it would be more a matter of sneaking unnoticed since there were two rather than seven and their mastermind in Garrek had been killed.

"They swap shifts on a third of the towers at midnight, we need to aim for the changing shift and slip past them when the men are distracted." Korx said with confidence and a tone lacking in any lenience.

"That would have worked fine as a plan when there were more of us, but if they do see us, we will be outnumbered faster since there will be four of them and two of us." Slint pointed out.

"We can take 'em." Korx grunted.

"We'd be fools to risk it. Instead, lets go before they switch shifts, that way the man at the end of his will be tired and less watchful!" Slint looked over at Korx, the older man was sharpening his blade on a rock and staring at it intently.

"Fine, we do it your way." Korx said again, stubbornly staring at his hands and pushing the rock harder over the dagger's edge.

"Well then we rest here until the moon is high, we need to be ready to catch our opportunity when the guard is concerned with something else." Slint appreciated the respect he was being shown, but it was done begrudgingly so his delicate confidence was worried for an outburst from his companion at some point. How much, really, could Korx allow Slint to lead them before he tried for the higher position, especially once they moved back into Barabel and he was no longer the least experienced of them. Slint needed to watch his back once they were nearer the barracks, he doubted Korx's ability to be the same once they entered their own lands.

Fellyn woke to Blake's hushed voice and Etana's beautiful giggle, a fire merrily crackling and the smell of meat cooking over the flames. She pushed herself up on her hands, weak and groggy from her long sleep. Blake looked over at her, his eyes danced when he saw her sitting there, ruffled and hardly awake and yet the most beautiful woman he had ever known. His heart raced and he grinned widely, unable to help himself.

"Good morrow my lovely lady, how did you sleep?" Blake asked with a twinkle in his eyes.

"Deeply. Is it early?" Fellyn spoke, her throat raspy from going so long without water.

"No maiden, it is almost noon!" Blake chuckled. "But it is safe here and the wind has let up some, we will eat and then journey on, it should take us no longer than another day to reach Callenham." Blake moved to where Fellyn sat and handed her the wriggling baby he had been holding. "Someone was hungry, I hope you don't mind but I allowed her to eat some berries while you slept, she loved them!" Blake looked at Etana and her beautiful ocean blue eyes twinkled at the sight of him, she smacked her lips loudly and reached for Blake's face.

"You...she ate food?" Fellyn asked, incredulous at his decision to feed her child solid food without her say so.

"Yes, she had some of those delicious berries we ate from the forest not a few days ago, only a few mind, since I thought her stomach might not take too much at once." Blake looked up into those perfect eyes of the mother who held Etana, they were fierce and full of power.

"You...decided to feed my daughter without me telling you it was okay to do so?" Fellyn's voice rose with the emotion in her voice, she had missed it, missed that moment when her child had her first taste of something other than mother's milk. "You took that from me?" She croaked, wanting desperately to wake up again and simply not to know this.

"I...I'm sorry she was hungry and we wanted you to rest." Blake softly reassured her. "If I had thought for a minute that you would be upset...I would have woken you instead..." He raised his hand to touch her cheek, needing to still the raw emotion that he had evoked. Fellyn flinched from his touch and turned her head, her gaze down on Etana, refusing to look at him. She felt a surge of guilt at her anger, but a need to be understood and a sad realisation that Etana was in fact not completely reliant upon her for survival.

"It...it doesn't matter." She spoke bluntly, wanting very much to get a drink and fresh air.

Blake saw her eyes soften once more and reached for the wineskin hooked on his belt, he handed it to her and she took it, whispering her thanks. Blake stood and walked to the fire, he stoked it and moved the meat that was roasting over it, turning it to prevent burning.

Fellyn sighed and pulled Etana close, needing to feed her so that her tightly strung nerves would relax once more. Once Etana had drunk her fill, Fellyn sighed and stood, she went to where Blake was sat in front of the fire and sat on his right side.

"I'm sorry, Blake." She whispered, he turned his head to look at her and smiled, incapable of any emotion but relief that she was no longer furious with him. "I...I don't like missing the moments that will be soon gone, my baby grows and will one day be grown...I need to cherish the little things and hold them tight so I never lose her." Fellyn softly admitted to him her heart's aching and inwardly cringed at how silly it seemed.

Blake turned to her and raised her hand, wrapping it in his own and found his heart once again racing at the feel of her skin below his. Blake's chest ached in longing to hold her and his mind fogged as the all consuming sight of her hand in his flooded his awareness. He wanted to admit to Fellyn that he felt the same about missing moments with her as she had described about Etana. He wanted to tell her that he was falling in love with her and needed to have her close, needed to have Etana with him because he was beginning to see the girl as his own and wanted so much to have it be that way. He could find no words to speak that could explain to Fellyn his feelings and so simply contented himself with smiling at her, and pulling her into an embrace that would hopefully translate all of that. She allowed him to wrap his strong arms around her, and with the arm not holding her daughter, she held him close too and breathed in, reeling at the wave of longing that overwhelmed her when she caught the smell of his skin.

Sid cleared his throat as he entered the little cavern, whistling a merry tune and carrying enough fruit to fill their packs.

"Sorry to interrupt, young ones, but if you're to reach Callenham soon you'd better leave within the hour, you'll need as much time as possible to reach the end of Valley Pass and then the trees on the ridge I spoke of, they will give you a place to rest tonight." Sid busied

176

himself with filling his own pack and then Fellyn's, ensuring they all had plenty to be getting on their journey with.

"Thank you." Blake spoke as he released Fellyn's hand, they had sprung apart at the sound of his voice and the heavy air between them shifted to an awkwardness.

"Where are you going now, Sid?" Fellyn asked, she would be sad to say goodbye to the man after all his help, her opinion of him had changed since the previous day.

"Oh I'm a traveller at heart, lady, I need to wander on for it is all I know." Sid laughed and walked to her, handing her the bag and patting her hand sweetly as he did so.

"You have been so kind...perhaps one day we can return the generosity." Blake said, smiling and taking Sid's hand to shake it warmly.

"Oho no! I am blessed for the company you shared, and especially for meeting this young lady." Sid bent to Etana and lifted her little chin to look into his gnarled face. "Mark my words, lady, this little one is like no other...but I cannot put my finger on why..." Sid smiled at Etana and then at Fellyn. "One day I'm sure I will be able to say that I met her when she was tiny, and be proud of you...all of you." Sid spoke kindly and with a confidence in their future, this once again roused curiosity in Fellyn.

While Fellyn strapped Etana to her chest once more, Blake went back to the fire and removed the meat that was sizzling over it. He carefully wrapped it in three sets of larger leaves that had been set aside and walked back to Sid, handing him the largest of the meat bundles and then went over to Fellyn to put the other two in their bag ready to leave.

"We ought to go Fellyn. Sid's right, we haven't the time to spare." Blake turned to Sid and nodded in gratitude. "Thank you again, Sidney

Bullrush, it has been a pleasure." Blake smiled widely and reached to take Fellyn's hand in his own, she looked down at his steady hand and placed her own carefully in his. She then hoisted Etana onto her hip and followed him out of the cavern entrance with a quick look back at Sidney. Luca had been lying by the threshold and rose when they moved to her, she shook her thick fur and followed them out into the cold passage with a bounce in her stride.

Fellyn and Blake moved on through Valley Pass swiftly, with renewed strength and zeal after their restful night in the cavern; which had easily been the best night sleep either of them had enjoyed in a long time. Blake smiled to himself and pondered whether it had been because of the fire warming their backs in the safety of the cavern, or because of the woman in his arms that he had slept so well. The sun was glowing down on them in its watery light of the fading autumn, winter was about to seize the land around them and enshroud them in the thick snow drifts that blanketed the mountains with the purity of a white sheen. Fellyn had Etana bundled safely inside her cloak against the chilly mountain air, but the wind was less fierce than it had been the previous day.

They trudged onwards, moving along the ever changing ground with its steep climbs and gentle slopes as it wound through the mountains. The path was well worn and beaten, hundreds of years of people using it to trade between regions and of animals moving to the southern side of the mountains away from the harsher climates of the angry snow drifts. They came to several points where paths joined Valley Pass, offering the decisions of where to follow to reach the elusive and well sheltered village of Callenham. Blake cast his mind back to the last time he had been home years before, his mother had been unwell and had filled his heart with fear for her health. Blake had found it too hard to look into the faces of his mother and Elenna, who were still living in the grief of loss, and the disappointment that Blake always brought when he returned home without the girls that the whole village had grieved. *This time*, he thought, *I am coming home with my*

178

arm around the prodigal child, now a woman grown. Blake was desperate to see the look on Elenna's face when she saw her daughter, and to see his mother too who would welcome her home like family because she practically was.

He cast his mind to how his mother would view his feelings for Fellyn, and how they would take to her new name. Blake decided to keep those quiet for a time since those factors might affect Fellyn's opportunity to settle home again. After all, learning her new name would only confuse the village folk and they would need to see her as she had been when the girls had been taken, not as the stranger she had grown to be. They would probably still see her as Blake's future sister-in-law...they would see Seraphia and would most likely be concerned with asking why Althia was not with her. He also wondered if they would wish it had been the other way, that he would come home with his long lost betrothed on his arm...Althia had always been the more beloved of the two sisters for her cheery personality as a child. Blake would show them the side of Seraphia they had never known, the Fellyn he had grown to love, and eventually they would accept how he felt for this mysterious woman and her new name.

Fellyn walked beside Blake, her arms tenderly stroking the lump in her cloak where Etana slept against her mother's chest. She tried to drag her blurred memory back to Callenham, tried to remember faces and names and the layout of the village. Fellyn could manage only what little flashes she had while on her journey, vaguely she could see the huts within it. The animals wandering the village, the river and trees. Turning to look at Blake, she thought about how it would feel for him to be finally bringing home someone he had searched for over many years...but she also realised with a stab of pain that it wasn't her he had longed to find, it had been Althia. Fellyn was confused by his easy demeanour around her, by his touch and attention which would suggest that he had feelings for her. Since knowing who she was, or who she had been, Fellyn had tried to figure out whether Blake's friendliness and comfortable way with her was purely because she had

179

been his dear friend growing up. She still battled herself over the guilt surrounding Jared's death, turning herself inside out and worrying the images of him as he died in her arms. She fought the inner turmoil that told her she was not worthy of being loved again and felt it would be best for Blake if she removed herself from him where she could.

Fellyn sighed as she realised she needed to ensure that she slept alone with Etana, no matter how cold their evening, it wasn't proper for her to allow him to lie so close while they were sleeping. She also realised she would need to restrain from touching his hands or reaching for him when she felt uncertain. Blake had so quickly become someone she needed, someone she could not imagine losing, yet she knew she would have to for his feelings were brotherly and her sore heart stood to be flattened when it all went too far.

As Fellyn and Blake turned a sharp corner along Valley Pass, they saw the end drawing closer to them. A thin covering of trees and bushes dotted their view, and Fellyn noticed the twinkling sunlight reflecting from a pool where the trees gathered. She smiled at Blake and they quickened their pace, picking up into a run as they got nearer and the playful edge to Blake overtook his gentleness as he began racing his companion. Fellyn slowed, laughing at his antics so hard that her sides ached, it had been a long time since she had laughed so much. They reached the pool and Blake stripped his shirt from his strong back and bent to the pool, dunking his head in the water and shaking the water from his blond hair when he emerged. Fellyn gracefully moved to the pool and pulled off her boots and thick stockings, she sat at the water's edge and dangled her feet in, shivering as she realised how cold the water really was. Blake sat, his chest heaving with the joy of running and from the shock of the cold water on his face. He reached his hand casually to where Fellyn's sat on the grass, but noticing his movement, she pulled her hand into her lap before he reached her. She needed to guard herself and her heart. Blake sat, a little confused but not wanting to break the ease of silence between them. He felt like he could just sit with Fellyn forever and need no words, they had become so accustomed to moving quietly through the forest that they communicated a lot through actions and expressions, but he noticed that Fellyn was avoiding his eye and his touch. Confused at her distance from him, Blake stood and moved past the pool to where several low hanging trees formed a secluded and shaded area.

"This is the place Sid spoke of, we reached it well before dark too." Blake spoke, needing some communication since Fellyn was avoiding him.

"Yes." Fellyn breathed. Her short response pulled Blake deeper into his confusion, so he simply sighed and moved on into the trees to forage for dry twigs and branches for a fire, it would be cold later.

Fellyn sighed and watched Blake shuffle around in the thick piles of leaves that carpeted the floor in a blanket of oranges and browns, she stared at his face which was screwed up a little in concentration. Fellyn's heart gave a little jump as she thought of him and his attempt to hold her hand, she had not wanted to pull away. Despite everything she had been through, the pain that was still fresh in her heart and the fear of being chased through the forest, Fellyn felt herself being drawn to Blake like she had never felt to anyone before. When she had been courting Jared, it had seemed so lovely and sweet to her, he showed her attention and affection that gave her butterflies. But Jared had never made her heart race at a simple touch, nor sent her head spinning with a glance from his eyes, Blake evoked emotions that Fellyn had no idea she was capable of. She shook her head gently to disrupt the spell that watching him had placed on her. It was foolish of her, a newly widowed and lost woman, to fall for someone she had no right to. Her heart throbbed once again when she thought of the sister Blake was really searching for. Fellyn told herself to stay strong and push him away, it would be better for everyone and Fellyn knew that as she was, she could not cope with an unrequited affection for a man such as Blake.

"Lost in your thoughts maiden?" Blake asked carefully, not wishing to further offend Fellyn, she was clearly already angry with him for his decision to feed Etana that morning.

181

"I suppose..." Fellyn said quietly. "Blake...what will they call me in Callenham?" She asked, suddenly very nervous at the thought of reaching the village after so long on the journey.

Blake paused, unsure himself what was right for this decision, after so long away from the village and living with a different name, what would be right for this woman of two names?

"I, too had thought of this. I think perhaps this should be your choice alone, for they all know you as the lost Seraphia...but you are Fellyn." Blake smiled at her sadly. He had piled branches and twigs into a pyramid and was busy rubbing them together to spark the dry leaves at their base. He stared at his work as he spoke and daren't look at Fellyn.

"Who am I to you, Blake?" She asked, staring at her hands which were entwined in her lap.

Blake looked up at Fellyn and sighed. "You are Seraphia because I have known you forever, you are the girl I chased through the village most days and you were there when we all stole apples from Mrs Green's gardens. You were there when we spent a summer's night sleeping under the stars by the stream and we talked about our dreams, you told me you dreamed of saving the world." Blake smiled at his fond memories. "I watched you turn from a girl to a young lady...and then lost you. I lived in a family grieving for you and Althia to return and then spent my life searching for you...both of you. In my heart you will always be Sephie. But you are also Fellyn who saved my life and who I have travelled these lands with. I know you to be both, but others don't...and they will be confused easily...but if you cannot live with the name Seraphia after all this time, then you need to choose now to be introduced as Fellyn because they won't change once you have been among them." Blake's voice grew more intense as he finished speaking, and as her eyes rose from her hands to his face, a spark rose from the emotion he had been pouring into trying to light the fire. Blake stoked the small flame and watched it grow, smiling as the fire grew and the heat ravished the cool and darkening evening.

Blake needed to tell her how he felt about her, that he could not imagine life without her now she was with him. He wanted to say that he had fallen in love with her and needed her and Etana beside him, but with all the loss she was facing after Tehya and Jared's deaths, he didn't dare do anything that might cause her to grow colder to him than she already was. As he grew the courage to say something to her, built it up in his heart ready to burst with anticipation, she spoke confidently.

"I shall have to be Fellyn then, I don't remember being Seraphia much, and I do not remember our youth or the marriages we were to make, I don't remember stealing those apples nor telling you about my dreams. I am Fellyn now, that is my choice." She returned her gaze to her lap and Blake's determination to speak out was thwarted by the mention of his betrothal to Althia. They sat in silence for a while, eating the cooked meat and watching the night draw in around them, the cold night reflecting in their icy spell of unspoken hurts.

Chapter 18 – The Dance

Slint and Korx crept silently past the lookout tower, cloaked in the darkness of the night and being careful to move where they would not easily be seen. The mountains had ended before reaching the border of Xandia and instead the flatter plains of Barabel stretched out before them, giving very little in the way of cover through which to creep. Korx shoved hard into Slint's back as the two stopped, a voice could be heard. Slint tilted his head and lowered his body to a crouch, looking to Korx and signalling that he ought to do the same. The changeover was happening, earlier than usual which meant that their rotating shift pattern was different than it had been before, they were in more danger of being seen now than any other time. Slint slunk backwards to a cluster of boulders and rocks, Korx behind him. There they waited and watched silently for the guards to change and the patrol of the border line to begin, here they would have only minutes to move out of range of the arrows and run into the darkness, hopefully the night would camouflage their passing. Slint waited until he knew it was his only chance, and with a nod to Korx, they sprinted into the black of the night, a shot cried out through the sky and an arrow sped past Slint's head, his chest heaving in relief, he pushed his body harder than ever in escape from the border patrol, Korx hot on his heels.

As the sun rose higher into the sky, Slint and Korx could see the tower of Barabel looming before them, its great walls and high turret pointing to the sky like a raised sword. Slint slowed, they had been running with only a few stops since being fired at when crossing the border and both had been fuelled to move faster, their hearts racing and muscles fighting to reach their home sooner.

When finally they came to the large gates guarding the tower, the day was well and truly upon them and the familiar sticky heat of Barabel's climate began to fill them with the dread of seeking out the Empress. Time seemed to race while his mind fogged, working out a way to explain their return without the girl, and fear coursed through Slint as he and Korx were led into a high chamber where she would be waiting for them.

After their usual morning routine, Fellyn strapped Etana to her body for the last time on this journey of theirs, she looked at Luca who was sitting by her feet as usual, waiting for their heading. Blake gathered what they needed to move on with, and a wide smile played on his handsome face as he looked at Fellyn.

"Let's go maiden, I think it to be high time you returned home!" Blake's excitement was contagious, and Fellyn's stomach fluttered with excitement and nerves. Blake led the party through a winding steep path up the sheer face of the mountain, they climbed over rocks and debris and Fellyn often had to rely on Blake's hand to help her scramble up the neglected path with the heavy bundle of baby strapped to her chest. Luca was anxious at the change of scenery, unused to the rocks and steep climb, she too needed help to be lifted up some of the more treacherous climbs higher into the mountain. After reaching a good height, their path led to a cave entrance, and Blake turned to Fellyn to see her reaction.

"We are almost there." Blake grabbed her hand before she could pull away and led her quickly into the cave, it was an extension of the path they followed but wound its way deep into the mountain itself. "These are the tunnels of Callen, they wind dangerously on many paths but only one is the way to our village. It has protected our home for so long, but the way through them has become the worst kept secret of Xandia!" He smiled at her, the confused expression still moulded her face and he sighed, knowing she still did not remember her home.

"Will it take long to get through to the other side?" Fellyn asked, concerned and frightened by the enclosed and dank space of the mountain's belly. It was cold and the damp along with a strange pungent odour that caught in her chest and throat.

"No, a few hours at most, but we will not rest now we are inside, it is sulphuric in here...too long inside and it'll hurt to breathe." Blake released her hand and held high the torch-lit branch he had lit back at their resting spot by the water, but it cast only a warm glow on the path before them. On and on they pushed through the tight cavern, Blake leading them through the maze of tunnels with confidence. They sat once when Etana needed to feed, but stayed only long enough to satiate her thirst before moving off into the unknown once more.

Fellyn watched the confident man beside her with an eager eye, relishing the opportunity to drink in every bit of him she could. Once they reached the village she was sure he was bound to move away from her, and like sap to loose bark, that would surely break a piece of her too when he did. As they rounded yet another bend, a light cast a warm glow onto the path and Fellyn's eyes stung from having grown accustomed to the dim lighting in the cave. Blake grinned at her, that easy familiar smile that crinkled his eyes and touched her heart, and they burst into the daylight and fresh air like flowers starved of the sun. Fellyn removed the section of carrying cloth that had shrouded her daughter's head, a protection from the sulphur and damp and Etana blinked in the bright daylight. Fellyn looked at the stunning scenery before her eyes and gasped at its magical beauty. Tall rowan trees lined the path into the mountain village, their leaves the colour of sunset with red berries covering their thin branches, their trunks splitting into many stems and twisted together like a the closeness of family. A river ran through the village, sloping down the mountain gently and babbling merrily in the afternoon sunshine. Her wide eyes tracked its path into the village and saw that it came from the most stunning waterfall nestled in the village's centre point, they walked through the tunnel of rowan trees towards the waterfall and Fellyn found that her eyes were locked on it whether she wanted to look or not. The water cascaded gracefully down smooth rocks and formed a spray of white at the river's birth point. They passed several huts which were raised high on stilts of differing lengths so that each one was rested on a flat and sturdy base. Heads appeared through windows and doors as they passed, until a small child flung herself from a door and ran into Blake's arms.

"He's home, he's home!!" The little voice chirped as she wound her arms around Blake's strong neck and nestled her head into him.

"My little squirrel!" Blake said happily, and he pulled her into a tight hug as he spun her in a circle. A woman followed the girl from their hut and came to where Blake now held the girl so she could touch his face and hair, they were laughing and talking in their own little world.

"Now now, Faye, Blake doesn't need to be climbed on when he's only just home!" The woman spoke with a smile on her face, she had hazel eyes the same colour as her hair, and her face was plain but attractive. "Hello Blake." She laughed as she reached in to kiss him on the cheek, he held her close, little Faye still in his arms. Fellyn's stomach jolted at the intimacy of their moment.

"Where's ma?" He asked of the woman.

"She's at home, we took her some broth this morn." The woman turned to where Fellyn stood and eyed her curiously, taking in the baby strapped to her body and the large dog at her feet. "Blake...you're being rather rude not to introduce us." She pointed out, Fellyn blushed a little at this.

Blake moved away and set Faye on her feet, smiling encouragingly at Fellyn. "I need you to call for a feast, Luella. The whole village, tonight!" Blake hugged her once again and ignoring the stunned expression on the woman's face, took Fellyn's shoulder and moved her away, practically running through the village and past the waterfall. Fellyn stroked the fence around it with her free hand and followed Blake through the long row of huts until he reached one with baskets of flowers dotted around the door.

"Home." Blake breathed, comfort washing over him like a sweet rain. He rose up the steps to the door and knocked twice before opening the door and entering, holding out his arm to encourage Fellyn to follow.

"Ma?" Blake called out.

"In the kitchen." Called a voice. "Is that my Blake?" Excitement radiated from her as she came around a door, a cloth in her hands and an apron around her simple brown dress. She had greying hazel hair and deep brown eyes, she felt familiar and Fellyn knew she remembered this woman even in feeling alone. The scent of the hut washed over Fellyn and her head spun as it brought a wave of memories from her childhood.

Blake hurried to his mother and wrapped her in a strong embrace; he swayed from side to side with his mother in his arms and tears swept down her wrinkled cheeks and into his grubby shirt.

"Oh my boy! You have been away too long!" She scalded him, pushing away and looking him up and down. "You've grown too!" She added.

Blake laughed. "Mother dear, I stopped growing about 6 years ago!"

"Yes and you've been gone most of that!" She scowled at him and batted him on the shoulder with her cloth, Blake winced as it hit his injury. "Oh, now what have you done?" She asked, concern in her voice.

"Nothing serious mother, a simple wound is all." Blake reassured, and as she patted his cheek, clearly not believing his lie, she looked at the girl standing alone in the doorway like an intruder on this most precious of moments. "Well now, do I know you?" Forey Cotterill asked, her eyes boring into Fellyn.

"Ma...It's Sephie..." Blake's eyes were gleaming as he watched his mother approach Fellyn. Forey stepped carefully to Fellyn and stared into her eyes. She reached her spindly hands to Fellyn and touched her cheek gently, breathing out a sigh as she did.

"Well I'll be...it is you my child." Forey's eyes filled again with tears of joy and relief, she pulled Fellyn into a warm embrace that brought tears to Fellyn's eyes too, she was loved and had been missed here. Forey pulled away and scrutinised Fellyn, her eyes resting on the wide-eyed infant in the carrying cloth.

"A child?" Forey asked, looking from Blake to Fellyn with eager interest. When Blake said nothing she clapped her hands together. "I think perhaps we will be needing tea." And with that, she turned and returned to her kitchen, bustling at the stove until she came away with a tray of tea and cakes.

"Sit, sit both of you." She ordered and they all moved to the chairs around the large dining table that took up most of the cosy room. "Blake, you should have brought her home sooner when you became a father!" Forey suddenly said, a twang of hurt in her voice.

Blake looked at Fellyn and smiled. "No ma. She isn't my baby. Sephie has been through a lot since she was taken...she goes by another name now, she has been Fellyn since she was found by a woman of the forest villages." Blake took his mother's hand in his comfortably.

189

"Well then...I'd like to hear all about it my dear." Forey spoke kindly to Fellyn.

Fellyn blinked at Blake, unsure where to begin. "I was raised by Tehya, who found me wandering the forests as a child. She raised me as her own in the village of Tebel, she named me for I had no memory of who I was. I married a man of our village and we had my daughter, Etana, four months ago. I left the village because we were attacked, and Blake and I...well..." Fellyn had to smile, their journey had been so unusual and eventful that she was at a loss for how to explain it to this kind woman.

Blake continued their story, they talked until the tea sat cold and only half finished, the cakes untouched as their story flowed from Blake like a revered tale of old. Forey had wet stains on her cheeks from the tears she shed while he spoke and she looked between them as Blake ended his story.

"What of Althia?" Forey asked, her voice hushed.

Fellyn shook her head. "I remember only a little of what happened. We had escaped the men who held us and were crossing a frozen river. I know that I was drowning under the ice when I fell in...but I have no idea where my sister is, if she escaped...or if she even lives."

Forey sighed. "I think I will spend the rest of my days thanking the Lord. Your return, even alone, is a miracle to us child." Forey smiled at Fellyn, she reached across the table to rest her hand on Fellyn's.

"I called for a feast tonight to celebrate!" Blake said cheerily, breaking the sadness at their story's end.

"Well then, you both ought to bathe before it begins. And child, I will try hard to call you Fellyn if you prefer?" Fellyn looked at the woman and her relief was written all over her face.

"Thank you." Fellyn said, and she took Forey's hand and allowed the older woman to lead her through the house to where a large tub sat behind a curtain, separating it from the simple bed a few feet away.

"I'll get the water heated dear." She said kindly and left Fellyn there, returning to her son who still sat at the large family table.

After his mother had sent for him to fetch water to heat for Fellyn to bathe, he had gone to tell Elenna that her daughter was home. Elenna was sickly and weak, had few joys left in her life and seemed to be in another world most of the time. She lived behind a veil of reality that protected her broken heart from the hard world that had made her incapable of carrying a child and then taken the two darling daughters that had been a miracle and blessing where she had thought she would never be blessed. After such a life, her husband had been taken from her with the dreaded pox which had robbed so many of their loved ones many years ago. Blake had been gentle with Elenna, expecting to find her either locked in her mind or just shrouded in her emotions as she was whenever the veil hiding reality was lifted. He had taken her paper thin hands in his own, he had told her that her precious Seraphia was home and had seen her eyes, clouded and unseeing, twinkle as the thoughts carried into her guarded mind. He had held her while she wept and he had told her that she was bathing ready for the feast that evening. After Blake had left, Elenna had washed and dressed herself in her finest clothes, ready to greet her child after so long apart.

Blake has then gone to Luelle's and bathed, since Fellyn would be using his mother's tub. His sister was rallying the villagers and helping to prepare the banquet of food needed to feed the village at short notice. Blake sat in the warm water, washing himself with the soap and scrubbing his hands clean ready for the evening he had been looking forward to since he knew who Fellyn truly was. Tonight he would tell her how he truly felt for her.

Fellyn stood in Forey's dining room, she pushed her hands down the pretty fawn coloured gown that she had been given to wear to the feast. Her hair, for the first time in a long while, was tamed in a loose knot at the base of her neck, several loose strands framing her face. The gown was long, fitted for a taller woman, but it gathered at her waist with ribbons pulling it tight into a crossed bow at the back. The sleeves were long and draped gracefully past her wrist. Forey moved away from the stove into the dining room, she smiled warmly at the woman before her, Etana balanced on her hip as naturally as if she still did so every day.

"Oh, darling you have grown into a beautiful woman..." Her voice was tender with reminiscence.

Together the three of them, with Luca happily settled by the stove in the kitchen, moved out into the evening. As they stepped from the hut into the village, Fellyn saw the crowd of people waiting to see her, she could smell meat roasting on a spit and in the crowd of faces below them, she found Blake's handsome smile. She looked shyly around the crowd and walked down the few steps, she took Etana from Forey's arms and holding her daughter, returned to the place she once called home.

Blake watched her from where he stood, his arm linked in Elenna's. Fellyn was stunning in a gown that skimmed her frame with the thin cloth, gathering at her waist and at her shoulders, the neckline low showing her beautiful creamy skin. She blushed a deep crimson as the whole village stared at her, checking that she was the girl they had waited to welcome home. They all took in the child on her hip and curious mutterings flowed through the villagers. Blake led Elenna forward, meeting Fellyn's gaze intently and smiling at her, he was sure she would read his heart from the look he could not help but give her, she was breathtaking. Fellyn looked to the woman on his arm and she stepped forward, intent on the pair in the crowd, slowly she walked to where they stood and smiled at her mother. Elenna raised her hand to Fellyn's face and touched it gently, her foggy eyes trying to find her lost child in the woman standing before her.

"Mother." Fellyn sighed, she remembered those eyes and her touch, remembering stories, of being held while she cried and being sung to sleep. The memories flooded her mind and she crumbled at the pure joy of finding herself at last.

"Seraphia...my baby..." Elenna's eyes filled with tears as she retuned to the world of the living, she saw the face of her child grown and beautiful, she saw all her prayers answered and her love brought home. Fellyn grabbed her mother and pulled her into her arms, both women's eyes pouring with joyful tears, crying for the years they had lost and could never return, for the pain for their loss and longing and for the bitter sweet reunion that they never thought would truly happen. As the moment faded, people crowded around Fellyn and her baby, talk broke out among the villagers of the story Blake had shared with his mother. The people were told of Althia, of Fellyn's new name and of the baby's story too.

The village was alive with the celebration of a returned daughter, they ate and drank of the best food they could find and all were joyful. Fellyn was herded here and there by those who wanted to remind her who they were, to ask many questions of her other life and to bless her for coming home. A woman her own age had come forward and grinning from ear to ear, had announced that they had been the best of friends as children and wanted to know if Fellyn remembered. She didn't, but she was grateful for the memories she was given all the same, and the lovely woman with a sweet smile and rounded face told her to come for tea as soon as she could. Fellyn was swept away by the humble homecoming she had been given, she longed to seek out Blake but she had barely seen him all evening, he, too was some kind of prodigal since he had been away for such a long time. The pang of jealousy she had felt at seeing him with Luelle had dispelled when her round faced friend, Katalina, had told her that was Blake's sister. Fellyn watched Luelle with those around her, she had the same easy smile and cheer that Blake had, with a similar glint of mischief in her hazel eyes but she was like their mother, where Blake was fair with his sky blue eyes.

Fellyn managed to find her mother once more, she was sat staring into the fire which roasted a goat on a spit, her eyes once more clouded. Fellyn sat beside her and reached her hand to Elenna's, she squeezed it gently and her mother's trance broke, she looked into her daughter's face and smiled again.

"I can hardly believe it child, forgive me...you have been gone so long I...I have forgotten how to be happy..." Elenna patted her other hand on their entwined fingers. "Tell me about that darling grand-daughter..." She said, looking over to where Forey was cradling the sleeping child and staring at her tiny features with wonder.

"Etana, she was born but four months ago. She had the cord around her neck and the labour was tough, the midwife said she will be special for it." Fellyn smiled, wondering why of all the things she could tell her mother, that was what she called to mind.

Elenna smiled, "You were a tough birth too, Sephie, I almost died carrying you." She smiled wistfully at her daughter. A silence passed between them before Elenna spoke again. "Your papa died seven years ago...I'm sorry he couldn't see you come home...he loved you so dearly..."

"Etana's father is dead also, I was widowed little over a week ago." Fellyn's voice choked as she spoke the harsh truth and felt a pang of loss for her forgotten father, but an understanding that they both shared the same pain. "I do not remember most of these people, mother I cannot bring them to my mind."

"You don't need to, they loved you as one of us, they will love you despite what you do or do not know." Elenna was a woman transformed when her daughter was there, her usual cloak of despair was raised.

"I hope so...mother, do you know more of Althia?" She was careful in asking, wanting to know but unsure what was acceptable talk after so many years apart.

"No." Elenna's eyes trembled at the memories. "I last saw her when the men came through our village. The day I last saw you."

"I want to find her..." Fellyn said quietly. Only now realising how she felt as she said it out loud.

"Blake has been searching for her since he was old enough to leave...you won't find her." Elenna said quickly, clearly wanting the subject changed.

"Is it true he was betrothed to her?" Fellyn spoke quietly.

Elenna turned to her daughter. "Yes, she was meant for Blake." Elenna saw something in her daughter's eyes that hinted at her true feelings. "You have feelings for that boy?"

Fellyn looked away, desperate to guard her heart again. "I...no, I was just widowed...I just wanted to know."

Luelle came out of the crowd where several of the men had gathered their instruments and had begun a merry tune, she grabbed Fellyn's hand and pulled her into the centre where several women danced to the music. Luelle led Fellyn in a dance that had them all laughing and singing along, Fellyn copied them as best she could and smiled as those around her joined in the dance. Before long, the men

195

had stepped in too, leading the ladies in formations and circles, lifting and turning them in time to the twangs of the lute and the cry of the cornet. Fellyn was dancing with a man who was most likely a few years her senior, he was staring at her like he had never seen a woman before, his thick black hair falling in a wave across one eye, dark brown and intent on hers. He made Fellyn uncomfortable.

"You go by Fellyn now?" He asked bluntly, skipping the formal introductions.

"I barely remember my past and was raised as Fellyn so yes, who are you?" Fellyn said with all the calm she could muster while dancing close to this intimidating stranger.

He smiled. "I am Hugo Wood. We would have married if you had not been taken, do you not remember me?" his hand around her waist pulled her in closer, she could smell his hot breath and trembled with the fear that his presence caused.

"No...I do not remember." Fellyn moved away in step with the dance, four of the ladies in each section of the dance moving together to form a ring or a cross by holding their hands together. They twirled in time to the music and as Fellyn's steps led her back toward Hugo, Blake moved so that it was his hands instead that met her when the ladies steps picked up again.

Fellyn's breath caught in her chest as Blake wrapped his arm around her back, holding her hand with his other as they had in the forest so long ago. The music faded to quiet in her tunnel vision, she saw only Blake and felt only him as they moved around the circle of dancing pairs. The song ended with a cheer, Fellyn's gaze broken by the sudden end caught her off guard and she clung harder to Blake, fearing she would faint.

"Swooning for me maiden?" Blake said, his face close to hers as he supported her, their noses close enough to touch. He winked at her, as if to reinforce his humour but Fellyn just exhaled, she had been holding her breath so long. "Enjoying the party?" He asked, slowly moving his hands to her arms rather than holding her as she steadied herself.

"Everyone is so kind..." Fellyn stated, her mind drawing a blank on casual conversation. She tried to concentrate on her feet and have them move in step with the music, but her mind fogged with the proximity to Blake.

"Except highly-strung Hugh?" Blake's roguish smile caused a flutter in her heart once more, she laughed and relaxed a little as his grip released her. She couldn't fight the temptation he posed, when she was around him it was as if all sensibility left her. Another tune picked up, a gentler song and one of the village women began to sing with the musicians, Fellyn recognised it as the river song, it was commonly heard in Tebel and Cabaro too. She smiled as she realised that some fond memory of her other home was also here. Blake swept her into his arms again, smiling at her tenderly as he moved her around the throng of close pairs. The singer's high voice told the tale of men falling for the woman of the water, of being ruined by her charm and magic.

From across the crowd of dancers, Forey still held Etana close, she watched her son with Fellyn, she could see how he felt for her. Forey smiled at the goodness of the Lord that he had given Blake someone to love after losing Althia, and for it to be Seraphia...she could think of no better alternative.

The night was full of laughter, but Fellyn found herself exhausted in Blake's arms. He could see her weariness growing and needed to speak to her before they separated for the night, when the blissful joy of the celebration would end and life as he knew it with Fellyn by his side would change.

"Fellyn, I..." Blake started, unsure how to tell her, where to start explaining to her what he felt when he had no words to describe it himself.

"I think it's about time we let this prodigal sleep, don't you Blake?" Elenna said in their ears over the music and hum of voices. She placed her hand on her daughter's shoulder, and turned Fellyn to face her. "Ready to come home, child?"

Fellyn smiled and nodded. "I need to collect Etana and Luca, my dog." She said, turning back to Blake, whose face was full of mingled regret and longing. "Thank you...for everything..." With in a tear in her eye, knowing what she was about to do, she kissed Blake's cheek softly and embraced him for a few seconds before breaking away and walking to where Forey stood in a group of chattering women with Etana. Fellyn's heart yearned to return to Blake and kiss him, hold him again, but Fellyn would not let herself feel that way now, *don't be foolish*, she told herself firmly.

The Empress sat, men lined along the walls of her chambers and her closest advisors around the table that filled the long room.

"How many men have we?" She asked, a flash of eager anticipation in her eyes.

"We completed several more dungeon raids in three cities, we are now thirty thousand strong your Excellency."

"Training?" She asked.

"They are but a pack of untrained hounds at the time, but they are brutal...we will be ready in a matter of days."

"Excellent. I want a message sent to Varose and whatever snotty little brat is running it." The Empress stood, her hands leaning against the dark wood of the table. "Tell them Darue was but a drop in the ocean of my might. Tell them I am coming for them." She smiled, stood straight and the men of her table stood also as she swept from the room, her cloak billowing behind her.

Chapter 19 – The Hardest Part

Many days had passed by in a whirlwind of renewing her memories of the villagers who loved her, cups of tea and stories around the hearth. Fellyn tried to split her time between the family she had just returned to and the villagers equally, but she was avoiding Blake for obvious reasons. She was frightened to allow him to get close to her, so her routine in the village did not include visiting him, in fact she ensured that he was not at home when she went to see Forey each day. Etana was enjoying small bites of meals now, her appetite large and her strength growing. Elenna was entranced by her grand-daughter, by her pretty little face and especially her eyes, so like Althia's. Fellyn was feeling more confident in her mother's health and wellbeing, she felt almost safe enough to leave Etana alone for a short time with her, perhaps soon but not yet. Forey doted on the little girl too, relishing time with her and sneaking sweet treats onto her tiny tongue when Fellyn was not looking.

Their lives had blended into the village as if time had not passed, as if she had never been gone and she found that as she met folk, her memories returned in snippets so she had some idea of what they had been to her before. She also found herself remembering Blake, mostly seeing him with Althia. She had memories of Althia sneaking out in the night to see Blake and then return before sunrise, they had only been young but had clearly been attached to each other and were quite the mischievous children. Althia seemed to have been rather like Blake in her playful and naughty demeanour, fiery and bold, Fellyn was more placid and calm so had not enjoyed their presence as much. She had remembered Hugh also, his gangly form as children in the village, she remembered Blake and Althia teasing her for their betrothal and remembered crying herself to sleep over it. How odd, it seemed, that here in this village such pressure to be ready for marriage was placed upon a child's shoulders.

"A penny for your thoughts, child?" Elenna asked.

"I was just thinking of my childhood here, my memories are coming back slowly." Fellyn smiled sadly.

"Let them be sweetheart, if I could erase the memories and choose to forget, I would." Fellyn's brows creased as her mother said this. "Oh darling not of you...of the painful times." Elenna reassured her.

"I wish I could erase Althia and Blake as children, it hurts to see them." Fellyn said in a hushed voice, as if afraid to be overheard.

"Well actually I wanted to talk about her." Elenna said in return. Fellyn sat up straighter, expecting another question about her feelings for Blake. "I lied when I said I had not heard from your sister." Elenna was staring at her hands, not daring to look her daughter in the eye.

"When...how?" Fellyn could not understand what her mother was suggesting.

"She wrote to me a few years back now, told me never to tell anyone but that she was safe and well."

"Where is she? Mother I need to find her, she belongs here with me, with us...and Blake." Fellyn's throat was tight with restrained sobs.

"She didn't say where she was...only that the men that took her were from Barabel...and that she was their prisoner still." Elenna sighed. "I wanted to send a party to search for her the minute I read it...but she told me never to tell or her life would be endangered...I think perhaps time enough has passed and if the good Lord brought

201

you back home to me, perhaps he will bring home my Althia too."
Elenna cried as she said her daughter's name, her face fell into her
hands and she succumbed to the emotion she had hidden for so long
over this.

Fellyn comforted her mother and shook her head, Barabel, a
dangerous land and forbidden for her to enter.

Rhia stood on the platform entrance to the High council court,
dressed in an elaborate gown of silver silk. Davey and Marcus holding
each of her hands and both boys as smartly dressed in black tunic with
white collar and tights under their shiny new black boots. Marcus had
a slight scowl on his handsome young face, he hated the city and had
been in a foul mood since they had arrived, and now he had been
dressed in fancy garb and asked to stand still and wave for a ridiculous
amount of time.

Cassius stood before the people, his hands raised and a large smile
comforting them, he had been elected as High Councillor after an
emergency vote. A rider from the watchtowers had come into the city
and delivered a scroll with the Barabel seal, it had been a declaration of
war. Since they were deliberating over their next leader, the
Counsellors rose a panic that they had no High Councillor to lead
them in battle and defeat the Barabel army. Cassius, as the younger
man and strongest of them was an ideal emergency vote, he was free
of the blame for Darue's murder and was liked by many of the
Counsellors and the people of Varose. Those three days had felt like
just moments in a whirlwind of dressmaking, visiting other Lords and
Ladies of the realm to gain alliances among the wealthy, and visiting
crowds to show her presence and support for her husband. Rhia had
been plunged into a social world she knew nothing about and was
shocked by the behaviour of the Ladies when their Lords were absent.
Their husbands were the wealthy men who supported the council and

so were away often to meet with them or to take care of their lands and those who lived on them. The Ladies held dances and social gatherings in their husbands' absence, enjoying frivolities and spending vast sums of money in a political bid to have a name as the wealthiest or most entertaining Lady. Rhia had heard rumours that these women took men to their beds as a man might take a mistress, she truly felt out of place here in Varose since her upbringing and everything in her blood told her that she needed not to spend her time with such women. That, however, was not an option. Cassius had made it clear that finances were not an issue now, she needed finery and exquisite taste or she would not be accepted by the Ladies, and that would not land him in good stead with their husbands. The Lords would be the ones to lead their armies, Cassius would need them in the war against Barabel, without them he stood to lose everything from his new position to his life.

As the crowds stopped their cheering, Rhia turned and took her boys down the steps and into the carriage that waited to return them to their fine new house. Cassius would be here for some time signing documents and discussing strategies of leadership with his Counsellors. The evening was closing in, Rhia needed to get her boys fed and ready for bedtime and needed to oversee the hanging of her new tapestries. After the first time she had entered their newly acquired manor house Rhia had felt it was cold and empty so had, despite not wishing to spend money frivolously, ordered the finest tapestries to be found or made and brought to her new home. She looked forward to helping the servants to hang them where she would like to stare at them and their hidden messages and stories, it would be the first comfort she would find here in this strange life.

Since war had been declared, Rhia was terrified that their new life living in riches would be cut down by a tragedy, and for the first time in her life, she feared that she and her children may be at risk of being killed or taken as they were now important political figures in Varose, like a beacon over her head it would draw the army of Barabel or ambitious Varosians to her. Tomorrow she would order her boys to be trained with defensive manoeuvres and to work a sword and bow. She sighed, if Jared were still with them, he would be who she would ask to do this job, knowing that he would protect her and her sons at all cost, but Jared was gone from her life now and longing for him was more painful than helpful so she shook away her emotions and stood to get out of the carriage as it stilled outside of her new home.

Rhia sighed, this was her life now and it would be so very different to how she had lived before, but as she walked to where Rowan stood at her front door to give him a message that would be carried to every village and town of Xandia, she realised that she could grow to love this life too, in time.

After delivering the message for Rowan to scribe, he said that he would arrange for as many men as it would take to have the message delivered throughout Xandia. Rowan bowed to the fine Lady before him and headed into the evening. Life as they knew it would be forever changed.

Blake had been chopping firewood to fill their store with, his brothers, being younger than he, weren't particularly good at ensuring their mother was completely catered for. He smiled, they weren't lads any more, both Samuel and Xavi were newly married to local girls, and had enough trouble learning to keep their own family happy let alone their mother too. *How is it*, Blake wondered, *that I am the last Cotterill left unmarried yet the oldest son.*

A smile flickered his face as he thought of Fellyn, he had barely seen her recently, she was being pulled all over the village by people who wanted to see her and talk again. Blake had tried several times to speak with her, but she was avoiding him, he knew it well but did not know why. He loved her, he knew that so well now, and he would wait because she clearly wasn't ready after everything she had been through, Blake would wait forever for Fellyn after he had fought so long to find her. He wiped his forehead on his sleeve and rose up the steps to his mother's hut. Forey was out, Blake saw her boots were gone and her cloak too, so he wandered to where she kept the cakes and helped himself, and walking through the house he went to where his clothes chest stood and pulled the sweat soaked shirt over his head.

A flutter of paper caught his eye as he shut the chest, a folded sheet lay on the chest with the large key they had found in the castle laid delicately on top. He took them curiously from the chest and turned the key in his hand. This strange key that they had been given when in dire need, yet had come to nothing and shown them no use when they needed or expected it. He opened the paper and read it, his heart in his throat as his eyes skimmed the delicately scripted writing, and then again to make sure of what he had read.

Blake,

I am so sorry to have to leave when I am only just home, but I cannot rest here without Althia beside me, it feels wrong to begin my life here again without her here too. I am truly thankful for you, you stayed by my side and risked everything to help me and you brought me back my life, Blake. I am forever in your debt. I know now who I used to be, and who you were too. I know that Althia belongs by your side and I intend to bring her home to you now. Please thank your mother for everything.

All my love,

Jellyn

Blake crumpled the letter in his hand, his heart pounding out of his chest as he ran from the hut and sprinted to Elenna's house, the key thrown to the floor, forgotten once again. He rapped on the door hard, waiting for her to answer but it felt forever before she opened the door to let him in.

"Blake?" Elenna asked, startled by his intensity.

"Where is she?" He asked, urgency ringing out of his quivering voice.

"She said she went for a walk, why?" Elenna questioned, confused.

"She left me this." He thrust the letter at her, she looked at his face and the severity of the moment, before undoing the paper to read for herself what had shaken Blake. She heaved her chest as the panic of losing her child again rolled over her, those clear eyes clouded over once more and Blake had to grab hold of her arms to steady her as she came close to losing consciousness.

"Elenna, are you alright?" Blake asked, feeling frustrated, he wanted to run after Fellyn but could not leave Elenna in this state.

"She's gone...I didn't think she would go there..." Elenna said in her trembling whisper.

"Where, Elenna where has she gone?" Blake took the woman's shoulders, he wanted to shake the answer from her but restrained, desperation fuelling his emotions.

"Barabel." Elenna said, barely more than a mutter.

Blake released Elenna carefully, resting her on the floor and fled out of the hut door in pursuit of the woman he loved.

Fellyn walked through the cavern with no light to guide her, Luca walked by her side and Etana's chubby little legs dangled down, her body tied once more in the carrying cloth. She would be too big for this before long. The smell of the sulphuric air made her throat raspy and dry and its stench turned her stomach. Blake had led their way before, and she was only vaguely confident that she knew the way at all. She turned and followed her instinct, trying to breathe fresh air to find her direction out the other side of the cavern but coming up with only the same smell of the damp walls around her. Pushing on through the tunnels, she realised she had no idea where she was, she reached a dead end and had to turn around, after touching the large rocks that blocked what once was a part of the tunnel system. She retraced her steps and took another route when she came to a fork, the tunnel was so dark that she had trouble working out where she had already been. It had been a long time since she entered the tunnel, her belly grumbled with hunger telling her it was late in the evening and Etana squirmed in communication of her own need to eat. Fellyn sighed and sat on a rock to feed the baby, she had only bread and cheese in her bag so until she found a place to hunt she would need to save the food for when it was really needed. After Etana had finished, she bundled her back up in the carry cloth to try and find the exit.

After a long while of puzzling the maze of tunnels, Fellyn's pace began to speed up and she found her breathing getting tighter. A dizziness clouded her mind and the walls seemed to be closing in on her, her heart raced and she started to panic. Her legs carried her onwards but her vision was fogged, she had no idea where she had been before and which way to turn. Fellyn was lost, hopelessly lost. Breathing hard and fighting to get enough oxygen, she felt herself sliding into an unsteady abyss; she slumped to the floor and wrapped her arms around Etana who was crying from her own discomfort in the horrible place. The sound of her daughter's cries penetrated her panic enough to cry out twice before her lungs were too tight to shout any more. *Please, God, help me find a way out.*

Blake was running as hard as he could, he had forgotten to put on a new shirt when he read the letter and his exposed back dripped with sweat as he strode through the tunnels of Callen. He followed his instinct, knowing the passages so well since childhood and was soon out the other side, he stopped to check for a sign of Fellyn coming through here but the rocky path left little in the way of a track to follow. Scrambling down the rocks and sheer cliffs like he did it every day, Blake covered enough ground to see their resting spot by the cold spring at the opening to Valley Pass. He stared at the sunset glittering from the water's surface and saw himself, too frightened to draw closer and be honest with Fellyn. He saw the way she had moved her hand from his grip. His mind returned to the feast, how she had tried to distance herself from him and yet she had been speechless and blushed as they danced. He should have spoken sooner of his feelings, he could see so clearly how she would have assumed he would continue to search for Althia. Blake knelt and rested his head in his hands, the clarity of her position in their childhood trio painful to think on. Of course she would think that he would still love Althia, he had never given her a reason to think otherwise.

"Please, oh Lord please do not take her from me now!" Blake shouted at the burnt orange sky. He stared up at the clouds, glowing as the sun radiated from behind their wispy shapes. He allowed himself a deep breath and as he felt his heart rate slow and calm, he heard Etana's cry from inside the tunnels of Callen.

Blake threw himself back up the rocky mountain side and surged through the tunnels once again, stopping here and there to find the direction of Etana's little voice, she had hushed for a while and he began to lose his bearings, but a small shadow came into view, tail wagging and ears pricked high. Luca bounced to Blake and shoved her muzzle into his hands, and heading in the direction she had come, Luca led him to where Fellyn sat on the floor, the baby wriggling in her lap. He rushed to her and pulled her into his arms, she was weak but awake and it took her a moment to realise what was happening.

"Blake..." She whispered, her voice hoarse.

"I've got you." Blake lifted her into his arms and carried both mother and child through the tunnels back to the entrance to Callenham and stopped only when he reached the river flowing past the rowan trees. He lifted her wineskin to her lips and she emptied the container, her thirst overwhelming.

"What were you thinking, leaving like that?" Blake yelled at her, his emotions raw with fear and relief. "I thought I'd lost you for good, Fellyn."

She looked at him hard, her concentration returning and her mind settling. "I thought...you need her..." Faced with his unbridled emotions she had no idea how to tell him what she had wanted.

"What? You thought you'd go alone to find Althia? I have searched years for her...and you, why Barabel, why now?" Blake shot at her.

Fellyn stood, she pulled Etana from the carrying cloth and breathed easier without the weight on her chest, she laid the baby in the grass with Luca and turned to Blake once more.

"She's in Barabel, a prisoner. You brought me home, the least I can do is bring her home to you." A note of sadness broke her voice.

Blake came closer, his emotions carving lines in his handsome face. "No Fellyn, you can tell me you're going all the way to Barabel to find your sister because *you* need her, but don't you tell me you're doing it for me. You are exactly who I need, who I have always needed. I have loved you since leaving the castle and I need you...Don't leave me now." Blake gripped her shoulders in his strong hands, staring into her deep brown eyes.

Fellyn was absorbed in his passionate words, she had none of her own, stunned into a silent calm in his broad hands and blue eyes.

"Do you love me, Fellyn?" He whispered, his eyes locked on hers.

Time seemed to still as the question he asked hung in the air, the emotion palpable between them.

"Yes." She breathed, completely at the mercy of the moment. A smile lit his eyes and spread to his whole face, he pulled her to him and kissed her passionately, drinking in every bit of her before the perfection of holding her so close was gone. They melted into the perfection of the moment, lost in each other's grip and carving a new world for their own. Fellyn didn't even try to fight herself anymore, nothing mattered but that he was holding her. She allowed herself to open to her emotions, felt the raw pain of their journey seep out of her troubled soul. She understood the forgiveness she had needed to feel for Jared, and for herself, knowing that she had not been at fault for his death. As their world shifted, the colour of the evening deepened, Fellyn opened her eyes to a brighter world, rich with beauty and loveliness. She exhaled, looking at the man before her. All that mattered now was that he needed her, and she him. He was showing her that she was loved for all that she was, in spite of silly childhood arrangements for marriage. Blake was showing her that she was enough for him and showing her that that she was *his*.

Blake stroked the hair from Fellyn's face, brushing it tenderly over her shoulder and he glimpsed the fish shaped mark once more below her ear, strangely red and raised like a scar. Curiously he stroked it with his finger and watched it slowly fade into a pale outline, as if it had never been there at all. He returned his gaze to hers and met her smile with his own. It was a new world he was living in, a better world and a more mysterious one with Fellyn to share it with, but a better one indeed.

210

Epilogue

Korx and Slint stood in the waiting chamber. They had been here all day, pacing the little bleak room waiting to be seen and sent to the Empress, they had news they had assumed she would want to hear but instead they were caged in like animals. Guarded by two men of lower ranks than they, the men were furious and determined to fight their corner when she finally graced them with an audience in her presence. Slint's anger had grown inside him, pushing away all desires to run and hide from the consequences of their failed attempt on the girl. As the daylight faded behind the slit window of the tiny chamber, one of the guards pulled back the bolts and opened the heavy door.

"She will see you now." He said, his voice level, unconcerned.

After a moment of confusion over which man would exit first, involving some mild shoving and glares, Korx left the little room and Slint strode out after him. Head high as if he were bringing great news rather than disappointment, Korx was first to be led into the ornate hall. Guards lined the walls and her advisors sat around the table she kept for control. Slint slipped in behind the second guard and Korx, he saw her thick dark hair and beautiful, cruel eyes, all the confidence he had mustered before fled his body. The two men stood before the table of the Empress, all eyes on them and their dirt stained clothing and disarmed sheaths.

"Where is Garrek, he led you did he not?" She asked them, a simple smile on her lips but not reaching her cold eyes.

"Killed, your Excellency, in a fight with the girl and her allies."
Korx said quickly, bowing slightly so he seemed to be doubled over
with pain.

"And the rest of your group?" She said, a false sweetness in her
tone that did little to dispel Slint's fears.

"Also dead, your Excellency." Korx muttered.

The Empress nodded. "Why is it that you are alive and yet empty
handed?" She spoke this time with warning.

"We came to tell you that she lives and where to find her." Korx
babbled, realising too late the danger he had put them in.

"Does it require two men to deliver a message, Korx?" The
Empress mocked him, her advisors murmured their appreciation for
the evening entertainment.

"No...your Excellency..." Korx stuttered, and seeing her nod to the
guard beside him who unsheathed his sword and turned to face Korx
head on, he shouted his plea. "Wait! There's more. A child, she had a
child also. A baby strapped to her."

The Empress frowned at him, her mind racing over the new
information.

"Thank you, Korx, you have been almost useful. Kill him." She
spat, and as she nodded at the guard once more, a sword was raised
and pulled down to slice his head from his shoulders. Slint held back
his revulsion as Korx's head thudded to the floor, the eyes rolling and
mouth agape. The Empress watched with a fire in her eyes, and she
turned her gaze to where Slint stood. He was suddenly grateful that it
was not he who had left the waiting chamber first.

"You. Come with me." She barked at Slint, and walked gracefully
around the table and down through the hall, as she swept past the

212

lined guards with Slint following like an obedient hound, a cry rose out from her guards until all were shouting in unison.

"Our Lady, Althia!"

A Note from the Author

If you have just finished reading Woman of Water, I thank you. I dearly hope the story touched your heart as it did mine while I wrote it. This story was inspired by a road trip to Abergele in Wales where my friend and I, along with my tiny baby daughter, sought to find God on the side of a mountain. We ended up in some incredible places with nothing but a tent and our car to shelter us from the wet Welsh weather. We camped beneath the stunning ruins of Gwyrch Castle and basked in its sheer beauty. This stunning castle and its derelict mysteries sparked my imagination and I found myself dreaming of Fellyn and her story sprang into my heart.

The sequel to this novel, Child of Ice, will be released soon and I really hope you will read and enjoy it as you hopefully did this one. Child of Ice continues the prophesy in a more urgent way as we learn more about Althia, Fellyn and Etana and what it really means to be borne of water. The story moves deeper into Xandia's secrets and magic, and our characters are faced with more dangers than they have ever known.

I would value your review on my work on the Amazon Kindle website, reading comments from readers will allow me to grow as a writer, and please feel free to email me at michaelabeckettbooks@outlook.com with any comments or questions, thank you!